STREET SMARTS

STREET SMARTS

John Woods

Woods publishing   Tucson, Arizona

This edition was prepared for publication by
Ghost River Images
5350 East Fourth Street
Tucson, Arizona 85711
www.ghostriverimages.com

ISBN 978-1-7338435-1-5

Library of Congress Control Number: 2019904888

Printed in the United States of America
May 2019

Contents

Dedication

To Ambassador Edward Dillery

An island of sanity in
a sea of troubles.

CHAPTER ONE—In the Beginning

Eleven year old Frank Grady awoke while Nurse Charley was taking his vitals. His mind was more focused, clearer this morning and he said, "How long I been here?

Nurse Charley said, "Three days and four nights."

On cue, Grandfather Jake entered and blowing on his cup of coffee, grinned at Frank, then looked to Charley and said,. "How's he doing?"

Charley smiled. "His blood pressure's down and his oxygen level is good."

• • •

Four days later, Frank was still weak but well enough to walk out of the hospital. "Grandpa, what happened to me?"

"After your grandmother died you were not looking good and went downhill real fast. I got you to the hospital. You had a serious urinary infection, your kidneys were shutting down, you threw up in the ER, swallowed some of your vomit and some of it got in your lungs and gave you pneumonia. You're a tough kid. How come you didn't die with all that going on I don't know."

When Frank was feeling stronger, Grandfather Jake took him to a quality restaurant. After putting in their order, Frank said, "Grandpa, you said you never cheated at cards. How come?"

"Morality is a tricky thing. One man you can trust with your wife but not with your money; one man you can trust with your money but not with your wife. Look and you'll see that morality skips all over the place, yet each man assumes that his morality is an absolute truth and carved in stone."

"I took pride in not having to cheat. Here's a lesson for you. A card mechanic I came to know confessed that he knew enough to win without cheating, but that it didn't feel right for him to win *unless* he cheated—like he didn't deserve to win unless he cheated. I felt guilty if I did cheat—he felt guilty if he didn't cheat. The end result was the same in that each of us would end up with the other guy's money in our pocket. Only difference was it took me longer.

I don't have much time left. After my heart injury I had to give up construction work, received a cash settlement, which I banked, and I then turned to the card table. If I was an accountant I'd be teaching you about accounting, but I'm a card player, not an accountant. So along with the only three decent books ever written on poker, I will be teaching you the how-to's of winning poker. What you do with that is up to you."

• • •

Grandfather took young Frank to a quality restaurant and said, "That lady and the younger man . . . you can look in his direction but don't look him in the eye. Now, what do you see?"

Frank looked for a moment and ventured, "Looks like the guy's doing OK."

Grandfather leaned back. "Ah! You're looking but you're not seeing. You think he's doing OK because she's smiling, but the guy's in over his head. He's a good-looking guy, the suit's okay, but look at his hands. He's someone works with his hands and he's smiling too damn much. He's trying to make out with someone from the upper classes and she's not buying it."

"How you know this Grandpa?"

Grandpa smiled. "Good question, tells me you're thinking. Notice how she's being upper class polite and toying with a strand of hair—she's being seductive—why?"

"I don't know."

"Because she's bored. The guy says, 'I like you' and she echoes back, 'I like you too.' Those three tells, her playing with a strand of hair, being seductive just for the hell of it, and turning into an echo station—that tells us she's too bored to bother saying anything even half-way original.

"I sold the house, got cash, no mortgage, and set us up with an apartment. You being the beneficiary of your grandmother's insurance policy, and you being the beneficiary in my policy, I set us up with a Joint Bank Account you'll be able to draw on after I'm gone. I've put provisions in my will that'll prevent your mother getting her hands on even one penny from my estate or our joint bank account. You'll be alone all too soon but financially you'll be OK, just don't tell anyone, don't flash money or buy expensive clothes. While I'm here I'll be giving you a head start, teaching you what I know about reading people, about cards, everything. Remember this, you can succeed at anything if you take the time to do things *correctly.*

Grandfather Jake was always watching. He said, "No shortcuts, be thorough."

• • •

Three years later Frank found Grandfather Jake sitting in front of the kitchen window . . . and quite dead. He thought, *Granddad was staring out at Mount Rainier. Today it looks like it's in our back yard.* Frank sat. After a time, he gathered himself, dialed 911, and reported his grandfather's death.

Before officers arrived, Frank took the role of bills out of Grandfather's pocket, and cut up his credit cards.

• • •

Tall and overweight, Detective Phil Baade was returning to Bremerton when he drove onto the Tacoma Narrows Bridge. Ahead, he saw a boy sitting up on the railing. Detective Baade stopped the car, got out, wrapped his arms around the boy and said, "You don't want to do this!"

• • •

On the locked ward, eight days later, Doctor Fyfe said to young

Frank Grady, "Your appetite has returned, medically you look good, and you're functioning well. How'd you know what to do when Weldon had his heart attack?"

"He was sitting behind me when he started snoring, I looked back and his eyes were wide open. I grabbed him up under his armpits, laid him down on the floor, hollered for a Nurse, and unbuttoned his collar."

"That was good, quick thinking. So tell me, how did you manage to end up sitting on that bridge railing?"

"When Grandmother died, Grandfather Jake and I took her ashes to the center of the Tacoma Narrows Bridge, said goodbye to Grandma, and poured her ashes into the outgoing tide. Then Grandfather died. I carried his ashes to the Tacoma Narrows Bridge, walked to the same spot where we'd poured out Grandma's ashes, poured out Grandad's ashes, and then I was all alone."

"Would you have jumped if Detective Baade hadn't grabbed you?"

"I was tempted to say the hell with it, but no, I don't think so... Slipping would have probably been more like it. I'd lost everything, everyone. I was totally alone. Was I hoping someone would come along? I don't know. This may sound crazy, but it meant a lot to me that someone cared enough to pull me off that railing and that the hospital would take me in. "That," Doctor Fyfe said, "Is not crazy. It makes all kinds of sense."

"God! I was such an ass getting up on that railing."

"Since you could have slipped, I agree. You have more than adequate financial resources so if we send you home, you think you could manage on your own?"

"I think so. I cook, Grandfather Jake knew he wasn't going to be around so he taught me how to manage a budget, bought me a series of texts on accounting and I sort of like hiding in those texts, I like the image of me being the one knowing where every penny is going. My Mom would love to get her hands on my inheritance. I don't like that . . . so suicide or screwing up by spending too much money is definitely not an option for me."

Doctor Fyfe nodded. "Detective Baade calls, asks about you. His wife is dying so he's either on the job or sitting with his wife. You have a lonely, rough road ahead . . . I'm sure of that, but I'll be signing your release and you will receive regular visits from Joanna Rosen, she's a psychiatric social worker, you'll like her, she's what we sometimes refer to as good people, and she's the one will be writing the reports keeping you in or out of protective custody, so you be nice to her."

Frank grinned.

"First time," Doctor Fyfe said, "I ever saw you grin. I won't kid you, you will have some lonely times but hang tough and you'll get through them."

"I don't want anyone knowing about my sitting on that railing and I sure as hell don't want anyone knowing I have money."

"Then don't tell anyone. Buy your clothes at the Goodwill . . . I can't emphasize this enough, you brag, you tell even one soul you have money or that you were sitting on that railing and the word will spread like wildfire."

• • •

Frank's family reputation was not good. His father was in prison for homicide while his mother had recently received parole, was on welfare, and lived on a barstool.

• • •

Frank was a strong, good-looking kid, and next door neighbor Adele Yonkey was Frank's age, pretty, wholesome, maybe not the smartest kid on the block, but Frank didn't care about that and asked her for a date. Solemnly, with what appeared to be a smirk, she said, "I would never date you Frank."

• • •

Frank was in the Navy when Adele, at age eighteen, was taken hostage in a bad marriage. She made her escape into the Navy . . . a year later, Adele said the wrong thing to the wrong man, they were alone, and he struck her with his fist.

Adele fell backward, her head thudded and bounced on the pavement, her whistling breathing stopped, and she was dead.

• • •

Decorated and retired Bremerton street cop Sven Sorenson, God-fearing, erect, and a vigorous seventy year old widower, after the death of his wife, had sold their Seattle home and moved to a rural area on the Peninsula.

The dark moonless night, followed by a clearing morning sky, held the promise of good early-morning fishing, so Sven hooked up his boat trailer and headed for Palmer Lake. He was taking the Croft Road cutoff, passing through the reservation's Christmas Tree farm, when seeing something in that early dawn light startled him! He hit his brakes.

His eyes had not deceived him. Sven Sorenson had discovered the naked body of Adele Yonkey.

• • •

Adele had been a slender and attractive woman with light brown hair. Now in bedraggled hair, chalky, blood-drained skin. She had been posed on her knees, legs spread apart, face in the gravel, and her left elbow was tied to her left knee and left wrist tied to her left ankle. These ties had been duplicated on the right side.

From the road, the first view of Adele was her naked butt and crotch.

That morning Detective Baade, who years ago had pulled Frank Grady off that railing, had led a night-long surveillance and subsequent early dawn raid on a suspected meth lab. With the booking of the suspects and paperwork completed, Lieutenant Baade entered Denny's Restaurant. Susan, his usual waitress, smiled and said, "You're later than usual."

"Earlier. Haven't been to bed yet."

Detective Phil Baade was rumpled, smoked too much, drank too much, and liked Italian foods. He was working his way through the scrambled eggs of his Grand Slam breakfast and looking forward to getting out of his damp clothes, into a hot shower, and then into bed.

His cellphone rang—not a welcome sound—Phil laid down his fork and answered the call.

The Watch Commander said, "We're stretched thin. You know Sven Sorenson. He's found a nude and bound body out on the Croft Road Cutoff. We need you to get out there and take charge."

Fatigue and chill were forgotten. Whatever else you might say about Phil Baade, you had to admit, he was all cop. So, driving with the heater on full blast, Detective Baade arrived at the crime scene.

Sven Sorenson, hands on hips, said, "A hell of a thing."

CHAPTER TWO—The FBI Interdicts

The FBI reopened the long dormant Adele Yonkey case.

Looking up from her desk, FBI Agent Kimberly Wheaten said, "Agent Huff, you're new to the FBI. Your record states that you rose to the rank of Lieutenant JG in the Marine Corps. What held you back from going higher?"

"On my 18th birthday I had a GED degree and I joined the Marines. I had put in seven years when I received my battlefield commission. With my becoming an Officer and my transfer to NCIS, I was spending too much time riding a desk. I belong on the ground, not riding a desk. I took early retirement and signed on with the FBI."

"Uh huh. You don't want desk duty."

"I do not. I appreciate being assigned to a high-profile case, but I'm an FBI rookie, a new guy, so why have I been assigned to this case?"

"The scuttlebutt from Quantico is that you are a genuine tough guy, that you are world class in firearms and world class in Judo, that you do 1,000 deep-knee bends each day that you don't run, and even unarmed, Frank Grady is a dangerous man. If and when we go to arrest him, we may need your gun or your muscle."

• • •

Huff tracked down Frank Grady's former boxing trainer to a bar on Tacoma's Pacific Avenue. Elderly now, and sighing with regret, Tug Thompson said, "Frank Grady—best prospect I ever had. World class, good reflexes, trained hard, always right there in front of you but not easy to hit, smart, cold, had a ton of stamina and was the most durable kid I ever saw. You couldn't hurt him with a crowbar. Quick hands, had a straight right hand with no hitches. He'd sneak in that straight right to set up the hook and then he'd damn near kill you with that left hook. Not much of a jab." Looking at Huff, Tug said, "You're a little bigger than Marciano, about 5'9," weigh about 195."

"You hit it right on the nose."

"Ever box?"

"Eighteen years old, my first tour of duty in Japan, I took up Judo. I'm a fourth Degree Black Belt in Judo."

Tug waved his hand dismissively. "I put Frank in with experienced amateur's right off the bat. He almost lost his first fight because he was staring out at the crowd or looking at me. End of round two he woke up enough to throw one good left hook and knocked the other guy down. He got up but was out on his feet and the ref stopped the fight. On his next fight he forgot the crowd, and from that time on Frank entered the ring focused and with that cold stare. He was unbeatable and peeled off sixteen wins and no loses against good fighters. You can buy me a beer now."

Huff signaled the bartender. "Frank was aggressive?"

Tug nodded, "Calm, cold. He stalked. Reminded me of Louis that way— if they wouldn't stand and fight he'd work them into the ropes and when they couldn't get away he'd cut loose on them. He was an assassin, cold, a good counter-puncher. You'd have thought he intended to kill the other guy."

Tug was lost in the memories of what could have been. Rousing himself, he said, "After Frank KO'd Stacy Kurtz, a spectator said to me, "The way he came after Kurtz . . .. Kurtz saw, and he was afraid. What do you feed a kid like that? Raw meat?"

$$\bullet \quad \bullet \quad \bullet$$

"When Frank's Grandfather died nobody wanted Frank. Then

he started boxing. That was when slimeball-wanta-be-managers, like roaches, started coming out of the woodwork.

"One of them, needing a shave and with cigar ash on his vest, said, 'You're a pretty good boy now. You come in with us and we'll make you a better boy.' Frank looked him over and said, "Fuck off!"

"Not," Huff said, "a very sociable kid."

"Not. But then . . . sometimes he'd surprise you. Once Frank came with me when I went up to Seattle to see my old friend Augy, a decent six round fighter, and like me, now retired. Augy volunteered at The Millionaire's Club where they fed the homeless. Frank and I watched as Augy dished out meals. Everyone being fed, Augy handed a sack with four stale doughnuts to an old guy with sores on his mouth."

The old guy cackled, "Christmas came early this year."

"Tug," Frank said: 'that old guy's probably not even fifty, and he's satisfied with stale donuts. If you're satisfied with so little, so little is what you're gonna get. I won't be satisfied until I have at least a million . . . maybe not even then."

Tug sighed, "Frank coulda been a champ. His last fight was with Sweet Charley Peach . . . he was a southpaw, had a great right jab and a good left cross. In the dressing room, he took to taunting Frank, said he needed to get ready for the Golden Gloves, so he'd carry Frank, for the first two rounds anyway, before knocking him out.

"At the bell Charley came out taunting and sticking with that solid right jab but midway through the round Frank had picked up on Charley's rhythm, was slipping the jab, and slamming Charley's right side with that wicked left hook. You never saw a sixteen year-old with that heavy a punch. Frank coulda taken Charley out but he let Charley off the hook. I said, "what the hell you doing?"

"I'm carrying him. I'll knock him out in the third round."

"Charley Peach was game but they shoulda stopped the fight. Charley came out for the second but every breath was hurting. Late in the round, Frank let loose that last left hook. You coulda heard it ringside when the ribs gave way. Even Frank didn't realize how hard he hit."

"Frank was that good?"

"He was that good. Charley Peach took a year off, then went on to have a decent pro career, and nobody ever again hit him with a left hook to the ribs."

• • •

"Where'd all that punching power come from?"

"Wide shoulders, deep chest, and the deltoid muscle was unusually wide from front to back. An older, bigger kid had given him a hard time so Frank punched the guy and busted his right hand on the bigger kid's forehead. The bigger kid was staggered, but recovering, he gave Frank a terrible beating—broke his nose and split his lip all the way to his left nostril. A young black guy pulled up, jumped out of his pickup, grabbed up Frank, drove him to Emergency and dumped him there. They reset the nose, sewed up the lip, and put a cast on the hand."

"What happened to the black guy?"

"Don't know. Frank looked for the guy, but never found out who he was."

"Uh huh. How did that relate to his punching power?"

"He read about old lightweight champ Battling Nelson who had a terrific left hook to the liver. Also, Nelson ran 20 miles every day. I don't know if Frank ever ran twenty miles, wouldn't be surprised if he did, but what I do know is he rolled up old stairway carpet and tied it to a tree behind his apartment. He worked out left-hooking to the liver on that carpet every morning—late afternoon he did it again. Three months later, he took up the double hook, left hook to the body, left hook to the head. His first two knuckles calcified, grew larger, and he grew calluses on those two knuckles. When his right hand healed enough that he could punch with the right, he joined my Boxing Club. Even the days he worked out at my Club, he still put left hand hurt on that carpet before coming to the gym."

"What happened to the kid who beat him up?"

"Cummings, Jumbo Cummings . . . way I heard it, when school started up in the fall, Jumbo hollered, "Hey Jailbird, how you doing?" Frank hollered back: "Hey fat faggot, how you doing?" Jumbo came after him and Frank slipped the punch, put two punches to the liver on Jumbo—and Jumbo was on the ground screaming in pain."

"A serious kid."

"Damn serious. I intended putting him in the Golden Gloves.

Then someone lodged a complaint saying that Frank Grady was taking on fighters out of his weight class, that Frank broke ribs, hit too hard to be a sixteen year old amateur, and that maybe Frank was older and a pro.

"By the time the Commission finished with their investigation, it was too late to enter the Gloves. Disgusted, Frank packed in his boxing career."

"He packed it in?"

"Yeah . . . and that surprised the hell out of me . . . He had money but at the time, nobody, me included, knew that. He was raggedy; with a flashlight, nights, he climbed into the Goodwill drop off box for his clothes. I thought boxing was all he had going for him. Later I heard he joined the Navy." Eyes narrowing, Tug asked, "Why you interested in Frank?"

Huff said, "He did join the Navy," "He could have jock strapped his time in the Navy but instead he was an accountant who also boxed."

Tug said, "I didn't think Frank even remembered me. Then, for each of my last three birthdays, March the seventeenth, Frank Grady has sent me a hundred dollars."

• • •

"What happened to Charley Peach?"

"Charley took a year off, then went on to have a decent pro career, and nobody ever again hit Charley Peach with a left hook to the ribs."

CHAPTER THREE—The Navy

Frank was reading a paperback when passing, USN Lieutenant JG Hays looked, read the title, 'Lust For Life,' and with his smirk in place, the Lieutenant said, "Looks good."

Yeoman Grady, looking up slowly, said, "I've seen prints of some of Van Goth's paintings, but not all. Never saw a Van Goth original. This is his biography; it's out now in paperback."

Grady didn't like the Lieutenant and turned his attention back to his paperback. Another Seaman was heard to chuckle at the Lieutenant's dismissal.

The Lieutenant had not been allowed to read his recent fitness report. Also, recently he had read a fictional mystery wherein the hero had discovered and thwarted his adversaries plot to plant sleepers, foreign agents, into the US Military. In this fictional account, male and female agents of exceptional ability had been planted in the US Military as raw recruits, where they would work their way up from the ground to a position of authority before being activated.

As destiny's child, the Lieutenant JG recognized that this fortuitous work of fiction had fallen woto his hands and that *only he* recognized the ominous implications of this supposed work of fiction, and *only he* possessed the acute perception to recognize Seaman Grady as a sleeper. Still, the Lieutenant knew full well that he would need to build his case in such a way that lesser minds would be able to recognize the irrefutable logic of his perceptions.

• • •

Having gathered his facts and suppositions, Lieutenant Hays requested an audience with Admiral Hollis. Audience was granted.

"Admiral," he said, "I have searched long and hard but have found no evidence that Yeoman Grady has ever had any high school, any college, any formal training in accounting, not in this country anyway, and yet his CPO claims he's a decent accountant. He's just now out of Boot Camp and already in process of receiving his first promotion."

The Admiral's eyebrows arose. Dryly, he said, "And?"

"Grady claims he has no family ties and that he was raised by his grandparents and they are now deceased. Suspicious, I checked with our Post Office. The only mail he receives is his monthly bank statement. I checked with his bank and I learned that Seaman Grady has over $32,000 in his account. A lowly and unrated Yeoman having that kind of money aroused my suspicions."

"Lieutenant, you have trampled all over this man's civil liberties. I find this unconscionable. But, with this now already in process, we will follow it through to the bitter end. You will notify Yeoman Grady that each of you will appear at this office at 8 AM tomorrow morning."

• • •

This Wednesday Seaman Grady, as he did every Wednesday since finishing boot camp, approached the gate to exit the Base. Checking his ID Card, the sentry said, "We've been informed that you might try to escape, make a run for it, and that we're to detain you."

This proved to be one more strike against Lieutenant JG Hays.

• • •

Admiral Hollis, said, "I was in attendance, front row, when a fellow recruit, who did not belong there, was thrown into the ring with you."

Frank nodded, "He knew that immediately—but he didn't run—I like to fight when it's competitive, but this was no contest. Rather than injure him I took him in a clinch, turned to the ref and said, "Let's turn this into an exhibition."

"So how did you fall under the view of Lieutenant JG Hays?"

"I have no idea."

· · ·

Frank began his accounting career and his gambling career in the US Navy, and while he was having his successes there, he was having no success when it came to snaring a girlfriend—they could see the loneliness, the terrible neediness in his eyes. That level of neediness, that much hunger, scared them. He bought a woman from time to time, but otherwise Frank saved every dime, every penny.

Frank had four years of service when he received his Navy Discharge. He had inherited a sizeable sum, and during his four years of service, he had made and secured another decent sum. Physically and financially, he was in very good shape, but emotionally, he was hungry, too alone, too needy.

· · ·

A cream colored Cadillac sang its Siren Song. Frank loved the way the Cadillac looked, the way it smelled, the radio, windshield wipers, plus (he thought) girls might find the caddy, and the one driving it, attractive . . . but Frank struggled free of the Cadillac's spell—and surrendered himself to the lesser temptation of a second-hand Buick—He said to the Buick, "Yeah, you got me."

· · ·

From San Diego, he headed north while hugging the coast. From Astoria Oregon, he turned inland to Vancouver Washington, jumped onto Interstate Five, and headed for Tacoma. Then he was hit with a terrible feeling of angst. He thought, *what the hell was so wrong about me?* I was a good looking kid, had a good body, and when I was all alone and asked Adele for a date she shot me down. Why?

He still hadn't found a girlfriend.

· · ·

Frank remembered Grandfather Jake saying, "I see others playing the weakest hands imaginable, in life and in cards, as if it's the courageous thing to do. I suppose you could call it courageous . . . but I fail to see what's so great about being a courageous loser."

Frank had made himself a courageous loser in love by letting others see his cards, his terrible neediness.

• • •

Arriving in Castle Rock, Frank had a change of heart. He thought, *everyone in Tacoma will know I'm still needy. So screw them.* He peeled off Interstate Five, looked at his road map, and headed East on Highway Twelve. Coming down over White Pass and through Rimrock, he saw two women, one in her thirties and the other a teenager, both in denims, backpacks, and with thumbs out. Frank stopped for them. He said to himself, *don't smile, don't ask them their names. That would say you're needy and want them.*

To the oldest he said, "Where to?"

"Yakima."

"Get in." A brief glance established that the girl was pretty. It was hard not staring, but not once did Frank glance in the rearview mirror at the girl.

The older one sat in front. None of them spoke.

• • •

They passed through Yakima, headed south on Highway 82, and half way between Union Gap and Wapato they saw a sign on a fruit stand that said, Pickers Wanted. Frank pulled in. "This what you're looking for?"

The older one said, "It is. My name is Marguerite Tyler. I'm Mexican and my husband was Irish American."

The girl leaned over the seat and said, "I'm Annette Tyler."

Frank said, "Frank Grady." He drove away pleased with himself. *It was hard to do,* he thought, *but I let them be the ones to make the first move.*

He had seen it in their and eyes. Both mother and daughter were hoping. Definitely, he had been doing it wrong all these years and it was clear that if Annette was out of those floppy denims and in a decent wardrobe, with the right makeup, if she took her luxuriant black hair out of that braid, it'd stretch down to her butt.

He thought, *She's not tall, but she's still a knockout and that girl will never need a hairstylist.*

She could be underage and he did right by not asking her age or looking her over in the rearview mirror. He thought, *finally, I'm getting the hang of this. Never let them see you as needy, as a beggar. It puts you one-down.*

Frank located the Casino in Wapato and was pleased to find they had a Seven Card Stud table. Seven card, after five card stud, was his best game. He checked into a local Motel.

· · ·

Frank drove back to the Fruit Stand on Monday. Marguerite was dumping her bucket of apples in the bin when she saw Frank walking down the orchard row towards them. Annette was up on her ladder on the other side of the tree. Margurite said, "Frank's coming."

· · ·

The three of them had dinner at a local diner. Frank said, "I've had a good week. So you order whatever you want and I'm buying."

"Why?"

"I've had a good week, picked up a nice piece of change."

"Doing what?"

"Playing poker."

"Sounds risky." Annette had still not spoken.

"My sitting in an air-conditioned room, drinking cool non-alcoholic beverages and playing poker, for me, is less risky than spending all day out in the blazing sun and up on a ladder swaying in the breeze."

Annette's mouth dropped open. "You're a professional gambler?"

"Don't you ever repeat this—either of you. How much longer will the picking last?"

"Sleeping in the weeds," Marguerite said, "it's tough. We've got maybe three more weeks of picking left. Then we don't know what we'll do."

"I was headed for Spokane when I ran into you two . . . those at the Casino will probably have seen enough of me in three weeks. I could give you a lift and you could probably find work in Spokane."

CHAPTER FOUR—The Coupling

By the time the women had finished with the picking, it was clear to Frank that they wanted him. Frank drove them up Highway 82 and over that treeless hump down to the almost treeless Ellensburg and then jumped on US 90 heading East and down into the Columbia Gorge. They crossed the Columbia River, then up into the flatlands of Eastern Washington. Annette said, "Momma, I have a toothache."

By the time they passed Moses Lake Annette's tooth was really bothering her. Frank pulled off Interstate 90 into Ritzville and headed for Ritzville Dentistry. The Office Manager was sixty years old, had sympathetic eyes, money-grasping fingers, and looking up she said, "Can we help you?"

"Take care of the girl; I'm paying for it." He handed the Office Manager a hundred-dollar bill.

Doctor Frohlich was a large man with a gruff manner. He shook his head—then performed a complete and thorough exam including X-rays. One of her back molars had an exposed nerve. Frohlich announced, "Saving that tooth will require a root canal. Otherwise the tooth needs to come out. I've had a cancelation so we could do the work now. Which will it be?"

Frank said, "Do the root canal. I'm paying for it."

Doctor Frohlich suggested Annette would probably want gas

and while she was under he could do other repairs.

Frank waved a hand, said, "Do it."

. . .

Coming out of the Dentist's Office, Annette was woozy. Marguerite walked her to the car and loaded her into the back seat—into the nest of her mothering arms.

Frank sighed, "The memories do come flying back."

Marguerite said, "You had bad teeth?"

"As a kid and all alone, all I had was money and I kept myself on a strict budget, way more than I needed to, and climbed into the Goodwill drop off box nights for clothes that fit. I practically lived on Wheatena when I could find it. Otherwise, I had oatmeal for breakfast and sometimes not much else. It broke my heart to spend money on a dentist."

. . .

Mother and daughter were big-eyed, silent, did not speak while Frank set them up in the Ritzville Motel. After securing his own room, he visited the market, purchased a newspaper, a pumpkin pie, a gallon of orange juice, and then, throwing caution to the wind, he visited the Rinky Dink Cafe and ordered three double cheeseburgers to go.

Annette pounced on the cheeseburger and then on a wedge of pumpkin pie. On finishing off her glass of orange juice, Annette's eyes began to droop.

. . .

Frank returned to the motel shortly after 1:00 AM. Hearing him drive up, Marguerite came to the door and said, "How'd you do?"

"Not too bad, picked up a little over two hundred."

"Wow," Marguerite said, "That almost covers what you spent on us today. Annette and I ate out of cans, slept in the weeds, and busted our humps for three weeks and you cleared almost as much in one night as the two of us did in working all day every day for three weeks."

"Let's see if you two can keep your mouths shut about what I do. Is Annette awake?"

Marguerite shook her head. "Even an earthquake wouldn't wake that girl up. You want my daughter I'll give her to you."

"What about your ex?"

"My husband's name was Fritz Tyler. We lived in Raymond, Washington. I shucked oysters, did janitorial when I could get it, while Fritz did odd jobs and auto repairs. He worked on cars at our rental home, buying junkers, getting them up and running, and reselling them."

"You were living on the poverty line?"

"We were. Poverty starved our marriage. We were worn out. Even with repairs the marriage was still a clunker."

"He leave you or did you leave him?"

"When I returned from the store the car for sale was gone, Fritz's pickup was gone, and the bench where Fritz kept his tools was bare. We weren't surprised, we'd been expecting it. We were evicted, left a yard and garage littered with worn-out auto parts, and worn-out promises."

• • •

The next morning Annette was out of her denims, wearing a cheap tank top tied up below her breasts, no bra and low cut hip-huggers.

Frank caught his breath. Her exposed belly was a thing of beauty. Her hair, being freed from the braid, was wavy, and being washed and rinsed, thick and shiny while cascading down Annette's back all the way to her butt. She stood and posed for his inspection. He nodded, extended his arms invitingly. Tremulous, she entered his arms.

Their first touch, first kiss, left her gasping, "Annette, I sure hope you're eighteen."

Her eyes sparkled. "I am and I'm ready for this."

"First, we pay a visit to Planned Parenthood."

• • •

A seaman from Montana had once stated that there was a poker game in the back room of every bar in Montana. Frank had listened, thought, *that's a big state and that's a lot of bars. Plus, there's the Casino's.*

Frank stated, "I like Casinos especially."

Annette said, "Why?"

"They're orderly, under control. We'll need to stop by Planned Parenthood, pick you up a decent wardrobe, and then we'll be heading for Montana."

Dropping her head, Annette said, "You'll take me with you?"

"I will."

Annette's head bobbed up and down.

• • •

Marguerite, Frank realized, knew more about second hand cars than he would ever know. They found a ten-year-old Chevy Marguerite judged was in decent condition, Frank paid for it, and the title was signed over to Marguerite Tyler. Clearly, the women thought, *we need him.*

• • •

Walking down the aisle of the department store, Frank's eyes fell on a tiny saleswoman. Her name tag gave her name as Jin. She was Southeast Asian and her wardrobe, jewelry, and makeup spelled taste and quality.

"Jin," Frank said, "I like your style. Annette needs a new wardrobe from the skin out and we want your help."

Jin selected, Annette modeled, and Frank nodded in approval.

Having new walking shoes, plus a pair of high heels, Annette giggled and said, "My first high heels, just call me Cinderella."

Jin called the luggage department and they sent down an appropriate traveling case. Annette, when attired in a smart new slacks outfit, visited the cosmetics department. She selected a makeup kit coordinated to compliment her own skin tones, and she definitely had a gift for applying makeup. Frank thought, *I knew she had a great body and nice hair, but I never realized she could look this good.*

Posing in front of the full-length mirror, Annette recognized a proud and devilishly attractive young creature. Annette said, "Wow," turned to her mother, and declared, "Someday Mom, we'll go back to Raymond, and those who put you and me down are going to eat our dust!"

Planned Parenthood was their next stop.

• • •

They took Interstate 90 East out of Spokane and Marguerite found employment at the first motel where she applied. Marguerite and Annette embraced and kissed while Frank started the car and the two women said their solemn goodbyes.

• • •

Leaving Spokane and the flatlands of Eastern Washington, they headed east into the forested Idaho Mountains. Annette relaxed her head on Frank's shoulder. Frank thought, *I can't get over how nice she feels. Annette's trust in me is breaking my cherry.*

"Frank, this is the first time ever that I feel like I belong, that I'm not just some half-breed beaner that slipped across the border."

• • •

The sun had begun its descent when they came into Coeur de'Alene. Frank said, "We'll stop here." The motel was modest, neat, clean, and featured a small swimming pool. To Annette, the motel seemed elegant.

Entering, with eyes expectant and aglitter, Annette came into Frank's arms. Annette's slacks and panties dropped to the floor, she stepped out of them, and leaned into Frank. He picked her up and carried her to the bed."

"My mother," she said, "warned me not to do like she did, give in to a man, get pregnant, and get trapped. Still, I'm Spanish and I always wanted sex."

• • •

The pre-dawn chirpings of birds could be heard as Frank came out of the bathroom. Annette was sitting on the edge of the bed, expectant, and again, she was ready.

Lying together, she said, "I've been scared of almost everything all my life but with my surrender to you I'm not afraid anymore. Thank you Frank."

He thought, *and for the first time since Grandfather died, I'm not alone. I thank you for that.*

• • •

After breakfast they shopped for swimsuits. On their return, Annette charged into the Motel and changed into her tan and thin-fabric one-piece suit. She slipped into the pool and Frank following, he said, "I'm strong and swim well enough to keep from drowning, but you, you're different. You are a true water sprite. You slide under the surface and then you resurface with scarcely a ripple. Annette, you are a true water baby."

Annette thought, *my surrender to Frank, it provides me with a comforting sense of oneness with God's Will.*

• • •

"Frank," Annette said, "who are your parents? Who raised you?"

"Grandfather and Grandmother; they're both dead. My father's in prison and my mother is now out of prison and lives on a barstool. Grandfather Jake taught me how to think, how to read people at the card table and on the streets. He bought me books on account-ing, taught me how to recognize when others are cheating, I had a gift for reading people and Grandfather nurtured it; he taught me about winning poker."

"Do you cheat at cards?"

"I can but I don't. Like Grandfather, my ego, probably more than my morality, demands I win without cheating."

• • •

After their third morning wakeup, Annette said, "Momma will be getting anxious."

They headed back to Spokane.

When they drove up they saw Marguerite pushing a cart down the second floor walkway. She cried out, "Oh, oh, oh" and rushed down. The two women hugged and kissed while Frank registered for two nights.

Mother and daughter visited the local Catholic Church and went to Confession. Frank, the agnostic, was surprised . . . and did not know what to think of this.

CHAPTER FIVE—Annette gets a job.

"Momma, I belong to Frank. I'm his, and God how I love it!"

Marguerite said, "And you Frank, will you take care of my little girl, and will you treat her right?"

"I will. Count on it."

. . .

"Annette, "I'm not one to throw around money. As a boy, when Granddad died, I had money, but that was all I had . . . so I was cautious, had a death-grip on every nickel."

"What about when you were in the Navy?"

"Ah. The Navy . . . in the Navy, for most, money was easy come, easy go. The revelation to me was that they enjoyed spending while I enjoyed having."

Nodding, Annette said, "You saved your money."

"Guilty as charged. I took comfort in watching my bank account grow."

. . .

They were driving about, looking for the elusive Casino, when they came across the State Employment Office. Frank said, "Let's take a look."

They looked up at the bulletin board and saw that in Ozon,

Idaho, the start of dam construction and the relocation of thirty miles of railroad track was underway. Laborers were needed.

"This is weird," Frank said, "Do I want this?" Frank registered with the State Employment Office, and signed up with the Hod Carriers and Laborers Union. He said, "Annette, I was looking for a cover for my gambling, and belonging to a Union just might do the trick. We're going to take a flyer at Ozon."

• • •

It worked. The Hod Carriers and Laborers Union was strong, and the guys already working were taking down good money. For the duration of the job, more than two years, they'd be working ten-hour shifts, seven days a week.

Mid-March, Hardin, the Contractor, walking down the relocated railroad track, looked Grady over, and said, "What'd you do before this job?"

"Navy."

"What'd you do there?"

"Boxed, had a ton of stamina and I never lost."

"Uh huh. You look strong enough to operate what we call a Woodpecker. The guy we have on it now isn't cutting it."

That first day Frank drove spikes for over a mile while developing blisters the size of half dollars on each palm. The next day he cut up a bath towel and wrapped the pieces around the woodpecker's handles. His hands would toughen, and Frank had the stamina and the athleticism that three days later prompted the Contractor to put another spike setter in front of him. He stayed right on the spike setters tails and took pride in keeping them hopping—Frank was putting the spiking ahead of schedule. A week later, after work and after dinner, he began hitting the gaming tables.

• • •

"Annette," Frank said, "I scoped out Freddy Schwab. He's the blackjack dealer in Bucky's Tavern. Blackjack's not my game but Freddy's a dealer ready for the taking."

"You think so?"

"Know so."

When Frank returned to their cabin, Annette said, "How'd you do?"

"Easiest $200 I ever made. I want to stay here for a while so I'll be moving from one game to another, most nights I'll win, and each night when I get up over a hundred, I'll quit the game. Annette, we have landed smack-dab in the middle of the Promised Land, a land of milk and honey,"

• • •

"In blackjack," Annette said, "my father told me that the dealer has the numerical advantage. So how can you win without cheating?"

"Reading the dealer. When Freddy will have to take a hit I don't hit my own hand if I have more than a thirteen. When I knew Freddy had a twenty I would damn sure hit my hand."

"How could you know?"

"Reading the dealer. When Freddy has a hand he will have to hit, he holds the deck ever so slightly towards the player, inviting him to take the hit and go bust before Freddy has to hit himself and go bust. When Freddy has a twenty he holds the deck tighter, closer to his chest, hoping they will *not* take a hit. Others will eventually pick up on this, so if Freddy doesn't wise up before they do, the table will go bust. I could tell Freddy or tell the others, but playing God is something I don't want. Also, my telling would be a brag and tip off some that I'm not someone to gamble with."

• • •

Annette talked to Ducky Martin at the Bigfoot Café. Ducky was a calm and languid-looking large man with sleepy eyes that saw everything. He reminded Frank of a fat spider—still, watching, and waiting. Ducky owned local properties including the hardware store, one of the motels, and the Bigfoot Café.

"Annette," Ducky said, "I'm putting you on days as a waitress."

Work on the dam was in full swing, Annette was in the wilds of Idaho, and rough and ready construction guys outnumbered the women more than twenty to one. Annette was the Bell of the Ball, sometimes worked a double shift, and those guys treated her with nothing but respect.

Frank ran that woodpecker ten hours a day, seven days a week. The blisters had turned to calluses, and months later, when the spiking was done, Frank switched back to the crew shoveling ballast ten hours a day, had dinner, and then would hit one of the games. Every bar and every restaurant had its game.

• • •

Annette was quick on her feet, remembered names, orders, always smiled, and no one gave her any crap. "In Raymond," she said, "people looked down on me and my mom. Here, they look up to me."

"Well yeah, you're friendly rather than seductive, plus you have nice boobs, a terrific butt, and the guys love seeing you coming and they love seeing you walking away. For sure, you're the complete package, a wonder to behold and they appreciate that, as they damn well should."

• • •

Mid-September, Annette said, "Frank, we're both working seven days a week. I'm worn out and you're a wreck. For the last two weeks you haven't wanted sex and I could use a good fucking. You're worn out . . . you're too tired to even screw. With no breaks from the physical labor, you still go out every night to pick up a hundred or more. The money's good—but you're about to fall apart and we hardly see each other. You're the boss—I'll do whatever you say, but it looks to me like it's time for us to fly away."

"Damn! You're right! Plus, I miss having time to spend with you. Would you give it another month? We could then take a long vacation, have lots of free time together."

"Another month?"

He nodded, "Another month."

"Okay."

• • •

Marguerite had been the Motel's Manager in Moses Lake for two months and was on the desk when Frank's car pulled in. Marguerite rushed out of the office and wrapped up her daughter in a fierce hug.

She looked over her daughter's shoulder at Frank. He grinned and said, "I'll leave you two for the time it takes me to get an oil change and lube job."

• • •

Marguerite and Annette took seats in the office. Marguerite said, "So tell me."

"Well—from Coeur d'Alene, Frank and I traveled north until we hit Highway 200 and headed for Ozon, Idaho. "I had made up a picnic basket with fried chicken, potato salad, three bean salad, ambrosia, we stopped for lunch alongside a tumbling small creek, and washed down our lunch with fresh-squeezed orange juice.

"I said, Frank, you want to get married?"

"I'm not against it. Do you?"

"Mom and Dad were married and that didn't work so good—I sort of like things the way they are—somehow, it feels safer, plus, I can always go to Confession and gain Absolution."

• • •

"So, Marguerite said, "This is what you want?"

"I do Momma, I really do. Look." Annette handed over her bank book.

Marguerite looked and her mouth dropped open. "You have over $3,000 here."

• • •

"Another revelation Momma, on the way here we detoured over to Walla Walla Prison."

"Why?"

"Frank wanted to meet his father. He was only five months old when his father went to prison."

"Oh my God! His father's a convict. I forgot about that."

"He is—and I like him—Momma, it was hot down there. After a year in Ozon, in that crease between the mountains, we weren't prepared for the heat down on the flat. We parked, locked the car, and entered the Visitors Gate. That place is noisy Momma."

Shaking her head, Marguerite said, "So. My daughter is living with a man who has a father in prison."

"Frank had seen pictures of his father but they didn't show the twinkle in his eye."

Margurite's jaw dropped. "He'd been in prison over twenty years, and he has a twinkle in his eye?"

"Uh huh. He's like that, upbeat and smart. He's not as big as Frank but no broken nose, no scarring, and he never divulged the names of his accomplices. Always, there was someone on the Parole Board who took a dim view of his reluctance to rat out the others."

• • •

Frank's father had been alternatively misty-eyed, then animated while, for the first time in his life, he exchanged words with his own son. Also, he drank in the picture of Annette and blurted, "Annette, to this old con you are a wonder to behold. I'm the coordinator for the Alcoholics Anonymous Program we have here, and there's always plenty of pruno, drugs and alcohol in prison but I haven't used for the last fourteen years. I play basketball every frigging day and work out with weights almost every day— and I will continue to carry the AA message of recovery whether in or out of prison. This is what I do . . . who I am. I have to ask you Frank, how much do you drink?"

"Seeing what happened to you and Mom, booze scares the crap out of me. I don't drink often and three drinks is my absolute limit. Annette and I have been making good money and neither of us could afford to let down even for a minute. We're going to take a long, long vacation."

David, looking at Frank, nodded and said, "I believe you. I was in denial, kept telling myself I could handle the booze, but I couldn't. Without the AA Program, in or out of prison, there is no way I could have got sober. Your mother was in lockup on a check cashing scam during her pregnancy, I visited her at Purdy Prison, and she told me she was so uptight she could've bit through nails. No way was that sobriety. For me, before I joined the AA Program, abstinence was absolute hell!"

• • •

The visit with his father had left Frank inattentive. Annette drove when they left Walla Walla, drove slowly, and Frank scarcely noticed.

• • •

Marguerite probed Annette about the character of Frank's father. She mulled over what she was hearing—then nodding her head she said, "Um." Marguerite began a correspondence with David Grady. Later, she would visit him at Walla Walla Prison.

CHAPTER SIX—Moving On

Stopping in Tacoma, Frank took Annette on a tour of jewelry stores and bought Annette a solid gold watch. Annette said, "But no one will know it's solid gold."

"Ah," he said, "but you'll know."

Annette purchased the ruby ring she admired before they headed for the lesser vacation area on the Washington Coast. The thought of solitude on a deserted beach appealed.

• • •

Outside Moclips they located a small resort, modest, quiet, and with a small indoor swimming pool. This late in the year the Washington coast resorts were almost deserted and it was there they met the statuesque Natalie Fisk. The resort was owned and run by Natalie's parents Carl and Rose Fisk. Carl was a big-boned man standing 6 foot 5 inches tall who had let himself go and was soft as mush. Rose was 5 foot 10 inches tall, plump, more assertive, and the boss.

The secret of Fisk success was niceness. They oozed niceness like a bad case of diarrhea. There are genuinely nice people and then there is—niceness.

Frank was familiar with Gavin De Becker's book 'The Gift of Fear.' Becker had stated: "Nice is a character trait. Niceness is a decision—a strategy of social interaction—not a character trait."

Carl and Rose Fisk constantly admonished their daughter, "Be nice." Natalie was eighteen years old and one inch shy of six feet tall—as tall as Frank.

• • •

On their evening walk on the beach, Annette said, "Frank, what's your take on Natalie?"

"What's your interest?"

"I hear things when I go to the store. What's your take on her?"

"Uh. She masks herself in denims that fail to conceal strong and fulsome arms and legs, a beautiful ass, and a good bust. Her face is handsome, more patrician rather than pretty. She has an athletic body, moves well, and could be a hell of an athlete . . .."

"And?"

"She's not. And her smile's a fake. She's one unhappy girl."

"What I'm hearing," Annette said, "is that the town thinks that Rose Fisk is a sweet-smiling monster who used her 'niceness' to castrate her husband and uses tears and niceness to dominate her daughter. Everyone agrees that Natalie is strong, physically talented, and a potentially dominant basketball player. At odd moments, they say, she surrenders and politely allows the other player to get off her shot."

"She surrenders?"

"She surrenders. They tell me that, last year, having another bad game, the coach pulled Natalie out of the game, publicly bawled her out, and said, 'Now you get back in there and let's see you play some *basketball* for a change.'"

"Natalie, getting her ass chewed, took charge in the second half, blocked four shots, took six rebounds, and was unstoppable. She scored sixteen points in the second half and that led her team to victory."

"And?"

"And Natalie's parents, having observed the coach bawling her out, decided the coach was not nice. Rose then forbid her daughter to play basketball for a coach who was *not nice.*"

"No wonder that girl drags around like a sick puppy."

• • •

"Frank, you'll never guess what I've found. You've got to see this."

Highway 109 ran parallel to the beach. Crossing the Highway, Annette had, in a damp spot, discovered a patch of carnivorous pitcher plants. They used their sweet scent to lure insects into their flowers, then devoured them.

Annette said, "We ought to put up a sign and rename them the Rose Fisk Pitcher Plants."

Frank nodded. "That's a thought."

"Should we?"

"It's tempting, but unless we're on the way out of town, let's not."

• • •

At dusk Frank and Annette watched the sun set over the Pacific. Their flagging libido's revived and they were never seen after sunset. Arising at daybreak, they would have an early breakfast and Frank would listen to the news while Annette puttered around in the kitchen;

Annette loved to cook, loved her kitchen.

They ran; Annette ran on the firm sand at the water's edge. When Annette had enough, she would begin the walk back.

Frank, before and during his time in the Navy, had regularly taken five mile long runs. Running that woodpecker, then shoveling gravel, had kept him in tip-top shape. Now, post Navy and post Ozon, Frank took up running in the soft sand high-up on the beach until his legs turned to lead. Then he would run back on the firm sand at the water's edge, allowing his legs recovery time while continuing to stretch out his lungs.

• • •

Natalie asked Annette to join her for an evening walk. Frank meandered along behind them while the two women charged ahead. Their animation and gesturing alternated with more solemn moments. On their return, the two women entered the cabin ahead of Frank. When Frank entered Annette said, "Natalie says she needs to get away from her parents."

Frank said, "Yes?"

Shaking her head, Natalie said, "I'm eighteen years old. I told my mom I needed to leave, that if I don't leave now then I might never leave. My Mom said, 'Well whatever could be wrong with that Dear?'"

Annette, looking to Frank and said, "She needs to get away."

• • •

Natalie was reserved, introverted, while Annette was extroverted and spontaneous. Yet, when together, each of them modified the behavior of the other; Natalie became a touch more spontaneous and Annette became more reflective—they were good for each other.

• • •

Natalie's parents did not approve of her spending time with guests and forbid her to associate with Annette . . . yet Natalie appeared at their cabin at noontime, looking wide-eyed and spacey. She said, "How soon will you be leaving?"

Frank saw the look . . . and decided. "Annette and I talked and we agreed. Your Driver's License," he said, "you have it with you?"

She shook her head.

"Go get your Driver's License and don't stop for anything else. We'll pick you up a new wardrobe."

Frank and Annette piled their things in the back seat. Natalie, wide-eyed, had her wallet, toothbrush, and basketball. She threw the basketball in back and climbed into the front seat with Annette. In minutes, the three of them were whaling down Highway 109.

• • •

Cannon Beach, Oregon was upscale from Moclips. Frank rented a two bedroom motel unit on the bluff overlooking the beach.

Then he received a visit from Cannon Beach's finest, cops Bert and Harry.

Bert said to Harry, "I think I heard a muffled cry. Did you hear it?"

"Yeah . . . I think I did." Looking at Frank he said, *"Step aside!"*

Twerp Bert went through the cabin while Harry was left to keep an eye on Frank, who was keeping his cool even though he felt like stepping on Harry.

Bert came out of Natalie's room saying, "The only thing in there is a basketball and a toothbrush." He demanded, "Where's Natalie Fisk?"

"What's going on?"

"We're asking the questions! Now where is she?"

"For Christ's sake," shaking his head in disgust, Frank said, "she's out clothes shopping with Annette!"

Bert located Annette and Natalie in the second of the two clothing stores. Muscular and almost a foot taller than Annette, Natalie was definitely not her prisoner . . . and the two of them were having a good time.

• • •

Then FBI Agent Pierce showed up. After interviewing Natalie in a private room he came out stating, "This is ludicrous, my being pulled away from Sunday dinner for a supposed kidnapping!"

Natalie's face was flushed. "I'm so angry! This cuts it! It's been a long time coming, but I'm done with my parents!"

Statements were taken, signed, and restraining orders were taken out against Carl and Rose Fisk.

Bert and Harry offered their apologies.

Frank, at this point, was only a blip on the FBI screen.

• • •

Meanwhile, myopic Alvin Frugate, a former classmate of Frank's, now with the FBI and performing administrative duties, had begun building a file on Frank Grady.

• • •

The day came when Frank was seated and both women took cushions to sit at Frank's feet and lean back against his legs. Natalie had never done that before. After a time Frank leaned forward and placed a hand on each side of Natalie's head, placed his chin on her head, and took in the scent of her hair. Natalie's breathing grew tremulous.

"Annette?" Frank asked. "Could this work?"

"We've talked," Annette said. "I don't know. I always wanted a sister, I put her on the pill, so take her into the bedroom and let's find out if this could work."

Frank stood and raised Natalie to her feet, and the tentative kiss became a gasping for breath.

Natalie was a big girl, would one day grow taller than Frank. He picked her up, she clung to him, and he carried her into the bedroom, Annette closed the door behind them.

• • •

When things grew quiet Annette entered and sat on the edge of the bed.

Frank looked to Annette. "Never" he said, "had I imagined anything like this."

"Frank," Annette said, "you're the one brings in the big bucks and you're the one with the big pecker so you decide if we should do this."

• • •

Ten days later, they decided, "This could work."

As a boy, Frank had stood defiant, alone, and angry. Now, Frank was standing tall and calm. Overnight, a lifetime of needyness and defiance melted into a quiet confidence. Strangers, at first glance, now recognized the calm authority shining out of the man.

Frank decided, "Both you and Annette have terrific butts so you buy bikini's. The two of you are making me the most envied and talked about man on the beach."

The women enjoyed being seen in bikini's. Both women were wonderful swimmers and in or out of the water they were a glorious sight. Their presence at the pool was much appreciated. Some who had not been near the water in years felt a sudden urge to go swimming.

Frank thought, *I always wanted popularity rather than contempt. Now with the two women I get grins rather than the curled lip. Be careful…this acceptance could be fleeting.*

• • •

"It's my dream," Frank said, "to settle down with the two of you in Las Vegas. That's where the money is."

Natalie said, "What would the two of us do there?"

"My formal education ended in the eighth grade but I never stopped studying. The two of you will either take jobs or go to school. Stagnation is not good, it breeds mosquitoes."

Natalie looked to Annette who said, "It's for us Dodo. He wants to provide us with a home and keep us safe while we build our own futures and our own bank accounts."

• • •

Frank was checking out Las Vegas Casino's while Annette and Natalie went house hunting. "Frank," Annette said, "we found a for-rent house we like in a quiet middle-class neighborhood."

"So tell me."

"Well, the house has two bedrooms, a great kitchen, big windows, and a neat yard with a shade tree."

Frank looked to Natalie. She said, "Also, there's an outdoor basketball court down the street."

They looked it over, Frank handed over the deposit and first month's rent and they moved in.

• • •

A group of young men met regularly to play basketball at the nearby court. Annette and Natalie wandered down the street passing the basketball back and forth on the way to the court.

Five young men, being short a player that day, invited the women to join them in a game.

Frank insisted that Natalie transition to the dominant mode while on the basketball court. In obedience to Frank, in games with good men players, she would get in their face and was competitive. All she had needed was Frank's directive and a figurative kick in the ass.

• • •

In the casino's, Frank eventually put together a win streak of twelve straight days, it had taken awhile, and signaled that it was time to move up to a bigger game.

At the gaming tables Frank came to know a number of mob Wiseguys. They asked themselves, *who is this guy Frank Grady?* They checked him out. His living with two women and seeing him working out with pro boxers, they saw him as a genuine, standup tough-guy. When an underling started mouthing off about a job, Frank quietly said, "Guys, do me a favor and don't discuss business in front of me—I don't need it, you don' need it, and if anyone rats you out I don't need you looking at me, plus, loose talk can get to be a habit."

Artie Karp put his seal of approval on this stating, "He's right. It can get to be a habit."

• • •

Artie was different from most Wiseguys, was Jewish, never swore, and attended the Synagogue regularly. Also, Artie operated from the back of the room, was a private type of guy, and a watcher.

Artie put out feelers to Frank about joining his crew.

"Artie, I appreciate, but I'm better working alone." There was a friendship between the two men that neither analyzed; as if ordained, it was simply there.

• • •

Annette was lamenting how much she missed her mother, when on cue, she received a call from Marguerite saying, "I just drove in."

Clucking in exasperation, Annette said, "Natalie, will you *please* hurry! My mother's never been to Las Vegas and she's stuck somewhere in the Wal-Mart parking lot."

• • •

Annette said, "Momma, there's no jealousy between Natalie and me. Neither of us is threatened by Frank's attention to the other."

That evening, after dinner, Marguerite said, "Frank, Walla Walla Prison wasn't that far out of my way, so I detoured, paid another visit to your father. He's looking good, spent more time asking me about his son and my daughter than he spent on charming me. He has beautiful wavy hair with a little gray and like you, he's sort of all muscley."

• • •

The following morning Marguerite lamented, "My daughter and I have been through some rough times. My husband woofed and barked about all the responsibility, did chest thumping about being a husband and father—but like all his other promises—he deserted us." Marguerite's eyes drifted across their faces." I came to Las Vegas hoping this threesome was working for my daughter, plus, I miss my daughter."

CHAPTER SEVEN—Doctor Melina Hamdi

Frank was entering real estate salesman Larry Osmund's hospital room while Doctor Melina Hamdi was exiting. She was tall, slender, olive skinned, and elegant. She stared Frank in the eye—and made no effort to hide her appraising.

Annette stomped when she walked, Natalie strode with purpose. Doctor Melina Hamdi glided on air and had an Arabic face that would have graced the cover of any glamour magazine. Frank stared after her.

Larry said, "She's Pediatrics, has no business with my gall bladder. She was here asking me questions about you and the two women you live with. What's going on Frank?"

"Beats me."

. . .

The sun was blazing through the windows but the air inside the hospital was cool.

Frank watched as Dr. Hamdi navigated the cafeteria with her tray of unseasoned and boiled-to-death hospital food.

. . .

During their evening meal Annette said, "Frank, you're not here."

"You're right. I've seen a doctor, an attractive Arabic woman staring at me. She's asking questions about me and the two of you and at this moment I don't know what's going on . . . but I'll find out."

"Who," Natalie said, "is she?"

"Doctor Melina Hamdi. She's finishing up her Internship in pediatrics, she's from Egypt, lovely but fragile, not physically strong like the two of you."

• • •

Seeing Frank's face, hearing him speak, others might suspect that he'd walked down some mean streets. Annette and Natalie appeared middle class, while it was obvious that Doctor Melina Hamdi had been born into the upper classes.

• • •

Frank arrived at the hospital cafeteria with two packets of gourmet food from Kusum's Indian Cuisine. The cafeteria was half-empty. Frank took a seat across from Doctor Hamdi and one seat to her left. He opened both packets and released the aroma of properly seasoned Middle Eastern foods. Frank pushed one of the packets over to Doctor Hamdi and began eating from the other.

Looking at Frank, Melina's eyes said, *clever man.* She smiled briefly. The food met with her approval.

When Frank finished with his portion of the food, he arose saying, "Same time tomorrow?"

Doctor Melina Hamdi hesitated, then nodded.

• • •

Doctor Hamdi took note of the enlargement of the first two knuckles of Frank's left hand. In response to her stare he made a left-hand fist. While tensing those first two fingers, the first two knuckles emitted a crackling sound. To her questioning look he said, "When I was a boy I boxed, in the Navy I boxed. My grandfather always said, 'It's better to do one thing right than a hundred things half-assed.' I have natural power in both hands, but as a boy and with my right hand broken, I focused on developing my left hook. Every day, left handed, I whaled on those pads . . . Even when my right hand healed, I was still focused on my left hook. This led to the calcification and enlargement of those first two knuckles. I had calluses on those two knuckles for six years. Now, twice a week, I work out with professional boxers."'

Melina said, "Boxing is barbaric!"

"That it is; and I'm damn good at it."

To his surprise, Dr. Melina nodded in approval.

• • •

When Doctor Hamdi took a seat in Dr. Weiss's office he said, "I'm told that you're being pursued by one of our local citizens. Doctor Hamdi smiled. *She was in pursuit of him, not him in pursuit of her.*

Doctor Weiss continued, "Some seem to think he's a gangster."

"That is possible. He's an athletic, well-muscled, dark-haired man with a sun-tanned complexion, has pale green eyes, a broken nose, and a scarred lip."

Doctor Weiss said, "We get our share of unsavory characters coming to Las Vegas. Is he one of them?"

Turning to look out the window, Melina said, "I don't know . . . but I'll find out."

Doctor Weiss cleared his throat. "Nurse Edwards was sitting at another table and looked over at the man sitting across from you. He recognized him. He reported seeing two plainclothes detectives having a Mexican leaning with his hands on a car. When they went through his pocket's they found drugs and drug money. Nurse Edwards said that the man he saw sitting across from you charged up looking like he was going to hurt the two detectives. He said 'Juan is a friend of mine so you two assholes give Juan back his money and *back off!*'"

Nurse Edwards reported they looked frightened. One of them said, "Sure Frankie, whatever you say Frankie!"

"Can you believe it," Nurse Edwards said, "Two big cops . . . and they were afraid of him!"

• • •

Curious, and troubled by this report, Melina asked Frank about it. With a shake of his head he reported, "They weren't cops. Juan does my yard work once a week. He had just cashed a big check and those guys were hustling him. I know them as hangers-on around the fight scene. One of their scams is posing as cops, flashing phony badges and planting dope on the mark. Then they scam the mark into giving them a payoff not to take him in."

· · ·

Frank had assumed he was doing the civilized thing by rising to the defense of a friend. Now it occurred to him that being socialized might have an inverse relationship to what he had thought of as being civilized. He mused further— *being socialized is surrendering to the norms of the society.*

This, to him, translated into his manner of rising to the defense of a friend had been an un-socialized act. He shrugged and said to himself, "*So?*"

· · ·

In the hospital's Conference Room, Doctor Robb said, "Doctor Hamdi, how did you come to know the scar-faced man who brings you lunch?"

"He brings me lunch. That is how I came to know him."

"I would have thought," Dr. Robb said, "his reticence to share his past would have been enough to alarm you."

"Somehow I find your intrusions into my affairs more alarming than this man bringing me a decent lunch."

Slapping his palms on the table and rising, Doctor Robb said, "I recognize Dr. Hamdi, that this man does not alarm you. And from this I must conclude that you are naïve." He then stormed out of the conference room. Doctor Hamdi shrugged and muttered a dismissive, "Pooh."

· · ·

Annette and Natalie were waiting when Frank returned from the Casino. Annette said,

"Frank, what's going on with you and this woman?"

"I don't know. What can she see in a street guy like me? Plus, she knows about the three of us. It's all a damn muddle with unanswered questions and it's got me damn curious."

· · ·

The hospital cafeteria was quieter than usual. "Frank," Melina said, "I hesitate to ask, but I'm off duty tomorrow. Could you take me to lunch in a public place where we could talk in private? Could you do this?"

He nodded. "You know about the two women I live with, yet you seem to have an interest in them and in me."

"Could you do this?"

"Saturn's Rings has a fine kitchen. I'll set up a noontime reservation for two. It's public and yet it will allow us to speak privately. Give me your address and phone number and I'll phone to pick you up."

Melina took out her pen and wrote her address and phone number on a prescription pad while saying, "Now I have to return to the Ward."

· · ·

Frank rang the bell for Melina's apartment. She responded, "I'll be right down."

In the Rolls Royce, on the drive to the restaurant, Melina sat quiet while adjusting to this new experience; this was the first time Melina had ever been alone with a man in his car—and this car was a Rolls Royce. "I drive the Rolls only when I feel a need to show off. I bought the Rolls from an entertainer who had lost big at the Roulette wheel. Each year the Rolls value rises so I'm keeping it as an investment."

When they entered Saturn's Rings the Maître De said, "Good afternoon Mr. Grady, and showed them to their table. The decor was tasteful, and the plate settings featured authentic crystal. Saturn's Rings was elegant, exclusive, and expensive.

The waiter consulted with Dr. Hamdi. She ordered the Fruit dish with yogurt. Frank ordered the shrimp plate.

Melina's facial expression was calm. "My coworkers and my supervisor wanted to know about the 'moves' you were making on me. It never occurred to them that it was me making the moves on you. They detected nothing, other than your having provided me with decent lunches of eastern foods, to indicate you were 'making a move' on me. Some seem to think you are a gangster."

"I'm not. I met Annette and her mother after leaving the Navy. They were broke and homeless."

"And you took advantage of their plight?"

"I suppose I did. I drove them to Yakima where they found work as apple pickers. One could also say they took advantage of my generosity. "

"They enticed you?"

"When they were through picking apples, I drove them to Spokane, Marguerite found motel work and gave her daughter to me. Annette and I then traveled to Ozon, Idaho, worked ourselves into the ground, but we made decent money, and were on vacation when we met Natalie Fisk who was being weighed down by the sticky 'niceness' of her parents—what I call 'smother love.' Annette invited Natalie to join with us in a polygamous relationship. This has worked for us. Our relationship is comfortable."

"This I knew already. It is one of the things that attracted me to you."

Their lunches arrived and Frank said to the waiter. "We would like to speak with the Sous Chef."

Sous Chef Annette exuded a sensuous self-confidence as she moved toward their table. She greeted Frank affectionately while speculation was in her eyes when she looked at Melina. She said, "What are you up to?"

Melina said, "Very soon, you will know."

Turning to Frank, Annette said, "You'll have to take something out of the freezer. My relief called in sick and I'll be working a double shift. Then Annette returned to the kitchen.

• • •

Scrunched up against the passenger door, Melina sat silent on the drive back to her apartment. Frank broke the silence saying, "On our move to Las Vegas, Annette was determined to find work in a gourmet kitchen. We had a plan. Preparatory, Annette had her Health Card in order when we began hitting the finer eating establishments. It was a stupid, crazy idea that worked. Saturn's Rings was only our fifth hit. We each ordered a different dish and Annette took a sample from each of our plates. Despite her being petite, Annette has a voracious appetite, but she doesn't sit still long enough to gain weight.

"Annette spoke to the waiter, asked him to convey to the Chef that she had her Health Card in order and would be grateful for the opportunity to assume a lowly position in such a fine kitchen."

The waiter returned saying, "The Chef would like to speak with you."

They ordered desert while Annette went to the kitchen and consulted with the Chef.

The waiter returned with a grin on his face. The kitchen had been short-handed and the Chef told Annette to put on an apron and report to the Sous Chef.

• • •

"Annette's a worker," Frank said, "and no dummy. Eleven months later she was a Sous Chef."

Melina remained silent.

"Annette had a poor beginning. She's great when it comes to her use of herbs and spices. Give her a taste of any dish and she can tell you each and every herb and spice that's in the dish."

"And Natalie?"

"As you already know, Natalie works in banking."

"How much of their salaries are they allowed to keep?"

"My early years taught me that life can be fleeting and so I've insisted Annette and Natalie secure at least half of each month's earnings in their own Savings Accounts. Usually, they do better than that. Looking at my face, it must be evident that there were those in the past who did not like me."

"Quite evident. The split-lip scar is more than ten years old, your nose was broken, and the resetting of the nose was lax."

Nodding, Frank thought, *She's ambivalent. She's looking to find something wrong, and yet, I think she's pleased when she doesn't.*

"Frank, what about children? Do you want children? Do you even like children?"

"Yeah! I like children—I like them a lot. We want children and we're working on it."

Melina chuckled, "I'm sure you are."

CHAPTER EIGHT—Melina Considers

Each Tuesday and Thursday Frank returned to the dingy and smelly pro gym where little was spent on upkeep. They used tin cans with holes punched in them for the showerheads. That's how they liked things, tough, gritty.

It was sweltering hot. Outside, they could see heat waves rising from the pavement. Inside, it was brutal. The air conditioner was on but not much help. Two days ago Frank had been in the bank when he noticed an inconspicuous and slight gentleman wearing an inconspicuous suit. The man had no distinguishing characteristics; there was nothing memorable about him—yet Frank thought, *I've seen this guy before—but where?*

Again, Frank saw the same mousy looking guy he had spotted in the bank. He was looking over hung-up framed newspaper clippings and pictures of old fighters."

After changing into gym gear and during his workout, Frank noted that he felt the presence of his shadow, even when not seeing him.

He sparred four rounds with Charley Braudus. Charley was taller, fifteen pounds heavier, and while both fighters are quick, it's Frank who has the heavy punch. Some, having seen Frank work on the heavy bag, were reluctant to spar with him. He's smallish for a heavyweight, just under 200 pounds, but he has a long reach and that ferocious punch, especially that left-hand punch.

Charley got careless and Frank rocked him with a solid left hook to the liver and a follow-up left hook to the head. That was about as dangerous as one can get with 14 oz. Gloves. Charley pulled him into a clinch while Frank caught his shadow turning away from watching the action.

Charley and Frank like each other, but on this occasion Charley applied his full attention to demonstrating he was the pro. By the end of four rounds Frank had been outclassed and hung out to dry.

Charley started on him again saying, "Frank, if you got serious, with your punch you could beat anyone you could hit, and that includes me, so when are you going to get serious and turn pro?"

"Charley, it's not going to happen."

• • •

After taking his shower and leaving the gym Frank saw the same inconspicuous appearing gentleman sitting in his car.

Frank didn't go to his own car, walked in the opposite direction, turned right at the corner, and halfway down that short block there was a recessed loading dock. Frank ducked in, out of sight, and waited. His shadow arrived on foot and Frank moved out and demanded—"Okay! What's going on?"

Startle hit the shadow's face, recomposed in a micro-second, but years at the gaming table had alerted Frank to even the microscopic expression of an emotion.

Frank's shadow, with the newspaper still neatly folded under his arm, reflected for a moment and responded, "You're Frank Grady. My name's Chuck Rose. I'm employed by Kellett Investigations and we've been retained by the Hamdi family."

Chuck moved slowly as he produced his Private Investigator's License. "The situation," Frank said, "has grown complicated. I suggest that we adjourn to a nearby restaurant. I saw you in the bank on Monday and you looked familiar. Had I seen you before?"

Nodding, Chuck confessed, "Being there but not being seen, that's what I do. Surveillance is a craft. Everyone seems to think that surveillance is from behind. Sometimes I stay ahead rather than behind. You surprise me. Usually I stay invisible."

"Huh, an Invisible Man. A sort of Peeping Tom!"

Chuck grinned, cocked his head to one side, and said, "Barney Kellett's new to this game. He did document searches for the government, I think he was probably good at it, but now he has started his own company and doesn't know what he's doing. He insisted I enter the gym and get in close where I could hear something. Left to my own devices, I don't make these kinds of mistakes. Working for Barney Kellett is amateur night."

As they walked Chuck Rose said, "I listened to the trainers watching your sparring session. One of them commented that the other fighter, Charley Braudus, didn't have the big punch and used his feet to make you miss and then countered you with quick combos. The second trainer said that you have a sneaky right cross and your left hook is the best he's ever seen. He went on to say that your body shots could make a fighter take a knee in a hurry. I'm unclear on what that means . . . take a knee?"

"When the fighter drops to one knee to avoid further punishment it's scored as a knockdown."

"The trainer," Chuck said, "went on to say you could be a good pro fighter if you didn't have money, he said: No fighter should be allowed to have money or a job. Money or a job ruins a fighter's ambitions."

Frank laughed.

They exited out of the side street and headed for the restaurant on the corner. "The coffee here," Frank said, "is passable."

"What I was hearing is that you have the punch and natural ability to make a name for yourself as a professional fighter."

"The last thing I want is to have is a name, to be known, it wouldn't be good for the women and I'm not about to place the management of my life, and the life of my family, in the hands of a fight manager."

Chuck and Frank arrived at the greasy spoon restaurant and took a booth. Frank ordered coffee, a tall glass of water, and two toasted English muffins with marmalade. Chuck was satisfied with only coffee.

Chuck excused himself to call the office and left his newspaper on the table.

Frank is an avid reader of people but when no one's around

his eyes will stray to the printed page. His eye caught the lovelorn column. Usually these columns didn't hold his attention. This one did—because the columnist, he noted, was *dead wrong*.

Returning, Chuck Rose said, "Barney Kellett will be joining us shortly."

"You invited him?"

Chuck shook his head.

"You didn't invite him, I didn't invite him, and so he's invited himself—arrogant bastard isn't he?"

Chuck nodded. "This is the first time—also the last time—I'll be working for Barney Kellett."

"This lovelorn column," Frank said, "you read it, then you tell me what's wrong with it."

• • •

The woman's letter stated that she had been seeing the same man for several years, that he was a good man, always ready to lend a helping hand, enjoyed the movies she picked, other events she liked, and they were campaign coworkers in their County Precinct. She lamented, however, that while she had a healthy sexual appetite, usually, he seemed uninterested. Sometimes, when she asked for sex, he'd get sarcastic, smart-mouth her, and complain he was too tired or didn't have the time. This made her feel like slapping his face. The two of them had sex no more than about once a month.

Frank said, "You have any thoughts on this?"

Chuck shook his head. He thought—*this guy's coming at me from an oblique angle. So what's he looking for?*

"This writer," Frank said, "Doesn't have a clue, doesn't recognize that this is a woman inclined to dominance, while the man is inclined toward submission and surrender!"

Frank raised his voice, "How about refills here?" The waiter, in greasy apron, looking offended and tight-lipped, refilled their cups.

Frank said, "Would you care to comment on the letter—and why I barked at our waiter?"

Chuck was cautious. He shook his head while eyeing Frank over the rim of his coffee cup.

Frank continued. "Those two people enjoy each other's company because each of them subconsciously recognizes the potential for acting out the primal fantasies that still lurk within our species. He's what we call a SAM, a Smart-Ass Masochist. He's someone who provokes abuse just like our waiter provoked me."

Chuck looked puzzled.

"Berne," Frank continued, "in his best-selling book, 'Games People Play,' written in 1964 and now long out of print, catalogued this pattern of behavior as the game of 'Kickme.' Freud stated that the fantasies of beating someone or being beaten by someone are the primal fantasies that people frequently use for masturbation. Beating someone or being beaten, even in fantasy, kicks our endocrine system up a notch; it therefore assists arousal. I sometimes run into these guys at the gaming table.

"There's a difference between laxity and laxity as a provocation. Our waiter's failure to give us refills was a provocation."

Chuck hid behind his cup of coffee.

"The SAM's of this world," Frank said, "provoke others to assume a dominant role. For them, it's a win, win situation. If they get away with their shitty little psuedo-aggressive acts then it's a win, and if they don't get away with it's an even bigger win—like when I jumped on our waiter—notice he didn't walk away slumped over, he stomped away with his back straight and his head held high. Masochist that he is, his receiving my figurative kick in the ass jump- started his endocrine system, kicked it up a notch. "

Perplexity registered on Chuck's face—then revelation. *This was a different way of looking at things.*

"This woman dreams of being the dominant one in the primal scene. The man kids himself that he is really assertive with his shitty little pseudo-aggressive acts. He made the first move, a helpless, whining and sarcastic provocation. In response, the lady reported she felt like slapping his face. For both their sakes, she needed to listen to that feeling and *do it*." Chuck's jaw dropped.

CHAPTER NINE—Melina's Father

Barney Kellett strutted into the café. He stated, "Frank, I have to go over some private business with Chuck and then I will need to go over some things with you."

Barney and Chuck took another table and put their heads together. Then Barney Kellett lifted his head, turned in Frank's direction, raised his arm and hand-waved for Frank to join them.

Frank ignored the summons—he stayed put.

Barney hesitated. Then, having no choice, he and Chuck came to Frank.

Once seated, Barney re-inflated his ego and asked various questions pertaining to Frank's Military history.

In the waits between questions Frank thought, *private detectives do not interrogate. They watch, they listen, record, and report.* Frank concluded that Barney Kellett had been watching too many cop shows.

• • •

"You're quite a guy Frank. "There's an incident report of you beating another Seaman so badly that he had to be hospitalized. How did you get away with not doing brig time?"

"That's simple enough. The guy was 20 pounds heavier, was a Boatswain Third, I was a raw recruit, and he tried to cold-cock me."

He thought, *Barney is able to access Government files. Interesting.*

"There's no record," Kellett said, "of you ever having been employed since your time in the Navy or when you arrived in Las Vegas with your pockets full of money and two live-in girlfriends."

Barney knew this was not true, but had also concluded that this untruth would somehow strengthen his position—Barney Kellett was grandstanding.

Sarcasm dripping from his lips, Barney continued, "I have to hand it to you Frank. You coming after Dr. Melina Hamdi, a member of a prominent Egyptian family, while still having the two floozies living with you . . . you sure have some balls."

Chuck saw Frank's reaction while Barney had not noticed.

"Mister Wassef Hamdi will be flying in here tonight. He has commissioned me to determine what you hope to gain from a relationship with his daughter. I have to say it would save us all a lot of trouble if you were to clear this up right now . . . you might choose to enlighten us as to what and why. Otherwise, I will turn your world inside out and I will find the answer to this question, either with or without your cooperation."

In poker, when a man makes a big raise, Frank will check to see if the veins in his neck are pulsing away. The raiser may control his voice and face but he can't always control his heart. If making the bet has caused his heart to race then the bet could be a bluff.

The vein on Barney's forehead was pulsing away. Frank looked Barney in the eye, sighed, shook his head, summoning up all the civility he had left, and said, "Barney, I suspect you were hired to gather the facts. But rather than gathering facts, you're attempting to build a case and with you as the star. You don't have a clue. Your attempt to panic me into coming up with some half-assed premise for going after Melina is pathetic."

Frank leaned forward and placed his elbow on the table. In a quiet voice he said, "Right now I suspect you have a tape recorder somewhere on your person! The weird part is—I don't give a shit!"

Chuck cleared his throat, said, "He doesn't have it Frank." He took a compact tape recorder out of his coat pocket and plopped it out on the table saying, "Nothing personal. It was just business."

Frank nodded. "Out of respect for Melina and her family, after her father has had time to recover from jet lag, I'll make myself available to Mr. Wassef Hamdi. He's come a long way."

The recorder was still recording. Leaning closer to Barney Kellett, Frank said, "Barney, you got away with it this time, but if you ever again refer to Annette and Natalie as floozies, count on it, I will put serious hurt on your sorry ass."

• • •

On leaving, Frank shook his head and said to the waiter, "You're a real loser, but you proved my point and I thank you for that." Frank left a ten dollar tip and the waiter received the tip like the slap in the face it really was.

• • •

The next day Frank received a call from Chuck Rose. "Are you willing to attend a 9 AM meeting tomorrow at Kellett Investigations?"

"Bad timing. I'm committed to playing in a big-money Poker Tournament tonight and that could last all night. Make it the next day and I'll be there."

• • •

The Meeting was scheduled for 9 AM at Kellett Investigations and lasted two hours. On leaving the Meeting and heading for the door, Frank thought, *Damn! I knew they'd be asking me to take a Psychiatric Evaluation. Why did I agree to submit to this?*

Then, behind him, Private Detective Chuck Rose chuckled and said, "Well Frank, you did it again; you took charge of this meeting as well."

Did he? Frank wasn't sure. Melina exited the building and called out to him. She approached. "I want to apologize for the exclusion of Annette and Natalie. That was unfair to them and if they will allow it, I would like to apologize."

"That would be good. Then you could tell them, me as well, what the hell you're up to. So give them a call."

She nodded, said, "Now I have to return to father." She turned and re-entered Kellett Investigations.

Frank walked a block before stopping dumbfounded and asking himself, *What the hell is going on? And why is her father being so goddamn reasonable?*

• • •

On Frank's return home, Annette asked, "How'd it go?"

"I don't know. I have a meeting with my tax man at 2 PM. Doc Frakowick will be calling to make an appointment. He wants to do a Psych Eval on me so take down the time and place. Also, you may be getting a call from Melina. I think we're about to find out what this is all about."

• • •

Doctor Melina Hamdi arrived by cab, paid the cabbie, took a deep breath, and headed for the door.

Annette, having monitored her arrival, opened the door and said, "Come in Doctor."

Melina was a head taller than Annette. Then Natalie entered the room . . . she towered over Melina. Natalie said, "We have tea, coffee, and baklava."

Melina thought, *so far, so good.* She took a seat at the table. "I would prefer Coffee. I like the title Doctor, but considering the reason I'm here it's too formal. I would be more comfortable being addressed as Melina."

"What," Natalie said, is your reason for being here? And this better be good."

"It is. Frank's grandfather had a damaged heart. My heart is more severely damaged than his grandfather's and I will not have a long life. Hopefully, before I die I will have time to have a husband, have a child, and after I am gone, I would like my child to have mothers and a father." Frank and the two of you fit the bill and I will set up Trust funds for any children I may have."

Annette and Natalie looked at each other. Natalie said, "Heavy." Annette, wide-eyed, nodded in agreement.

"There was no way to drop this on you gently. Frank doesn't know it yet." Taking a bite of baklava Melina paused and said, "This is very good."

"I make baklava," Annette said, "fairly regularly,"

Melina nodded, "So you bake too."

"Oh yes. This has got serious . . . so tell us, how did Frank do at the meeting?"

Melina sat down her baklava, wiped the crumbs from her lips, legs crossed, she leaned forward, and said, "You would have been proud of him. He walked into that meeting at precisely 9 AM and commandeered the seat directly across from my father. One could have expected him to feel defensive but he was calm and unapologetic about his living with the two of you."

Natalie said, "And you didn't find that strange?"

"I found it daring. Most men, I think, may dream of having more than one woman in their life but, in this society, they may not . . . not publicly anyway. Yet I think Frank would risk doing what other men only dream of doing and do it well. My supervisor has declared that my joining into an already established ménage would be professional suicide."

"Uh huh," Natalie said, "And what do you think?"

Melina shrugged, "Pooh. There will always be a need for doctors and I will practice medicine for as long as I am able."

Natalie echoed, "as long as you're able. Annette and I encounter curiosity, and sometimes a grin and a raised eyebrow. But with what you just confessed, well, it takes my breath away."

"How do you think Frank will respond to my revelations?"

It was Annette who said, "He's at his best when the going gets tough and even with you being damaged, you are still a prize. So! Melina, what happened at that meeting?"

"The men were acting as if I wasn't even there, which was ludicrous since this was all about me. The room was well lit, had a table and three chairs on each side and a chair at each end. My father was in the middle seat on one side, Barney Kellett was seated at father's left, and Chuck Rose was seated at father's right. Doctor Frakowick was seated at the table end closest to the door and I was seated at the far end of the table but as an observer rather than a participant."

"Only as an observer," Natalie said, "placed in a submissive role. How did Frank respond to that?"

"That was curious. He had a funny look on his face, acknowledged my presence with a nod, didn't speak, and took the chair directly across from my father. The men had copies of the reports from Kellett Investigations in front of them. I think the men's strategy was to unnerve Frank while they pored over the reports. Frank leaned back, crossed his arms and closed his eyes." Smiling at the memory, Melina continued, "So much for intimidating him. When my father finished with his review he set the reports down and coughed. Frank's eyes opened and looking across the table he said, "I take it you are Mr. Wassef Hamdi?"

"I am."

Frank then stared at Dr. Frakowick with an intensity that could only be defined as feral. It was beyond all social convention. Quietly, he said, "Who the hell are you?"

He replied, "I'm Doctor Frakowick."

Frank said, "Psychiatrist?"

"I am."

"Are you a Certified Psychoanalyst?"

"I am."

"Do you work as a consultant to the Police Department?"

"On occasion."

"Are you familiar with the work of Samenow and Yokelson?"

Dr. Frakowich's eyes went wide. He declared, "I am."

"Would you be willing to define what significant factor limited and profoundly influenced the scope of their investigations?"

Frakowick didn't flinch under Frank's baleful eye. He replied, "Why don't you tell me?"

Frank nodded. "I submit that in work with offenders one must concentrate on the objective and specific attitudes prevalent within that population—criminal pride being the most obvious. Samenow and Yokelson avoided addressing issues specific only to the individual—lest they leave that individual vulnerable to manipulation or pressure from his peers.

Dr. Frakowick nodded in agreement—*or was it approval?*

Frank then asked Dr. Frakowick if he was familiar with the theories of Dr. Robert Langs.

Again, Dr. Frakowick said, "I am."

"What is the consequence of Langs insistence on always securing the frame?"

Dr. Frakowick leaned back, apparently enjoying himself, and said, "So tell me?"

Frank laughed and the feral intensity of his scrutiny faded. Dr. Frakowick had passed Frank's inspection. He said, "You're putting it back on me aren't you Doc? Okay. Langs insistence on submission and compliance, what he calls securing the frame— obeying the protocols—is the therapist functioning as the patient's critical superego. I suspect that, more often than not, it drives them right out of treatment.

Frakowick said, "Amazing! You're a lay person, yet you're well-read and have arrived at conclusions that have evaded many in my own profession. If not for this immediate issue I would enjoy continuing this dialog."

"Freud's daughter Anna reported that creativity will sometimes overcome poor training. Fortunately, I had no training, poor or otherwise, to overcome. I can read and think critically and I've always been curious."

"Does sound like Frank," Annette said."

Melina took a sip of coffee, sat down her cup, and leaned forward. "I am a well-educated woman and Frank's response will always be with me. That statement mirrored iconoclasm in its purest form. And yet he was not through telling it like it is.

"Tight-lipped and angry, Frank said, 'Now you look around this room Doctor—and then you tell me—what in the hell is wrong with this picture?'"

"I jumped, was startled, I think we all were, by Frank's suddenly visible anger and it became clear that this was not a man to be trifled with. Dr. Frakowick looked around the room, nodded, and announced, 'There's an empty chair on each side of you—two significant parties to this drama are missing.'"

Frank nodded, "Annette Tyler and Natalie Fisk. Their exclusion from this meeting is a statement that their interests, even their worth, may be discounted, that they're expendable—I won't have it! They should have been invited to sit at this table and participate in this meeting. Failure to invite them is an insult. Neglecting to provide Doctor Melina Hamdi with a copy of those reports you all found so damn interesting is also an insult!"

Nodding, Natalie said, "Now you know. The fire in this man burns hot, and Frank is a bit of a thug. Pity the poor SOB who tries to harm any of us."

Melina nodded, "My father's eyes went wide. For the first time I detected the light of approval in my father's eyes—Frank's expression of loyalty to the two of you had gained my father's approval and my father declared, 'Frank, if my daughter entered into a relationship with you, how would my daughter's relationship differ from the relationships you have with Annette and Natalie?'"

Turning to Barney Kellett, Frank said, "You should have informed Mister Hamdi that the relationships I have with Annette and Natalie were fully negotiated."

"I would have, if I'd believed it."

"So, you decided that Mr. Hamdi needed the protection of your wise discretion."

"I feel that is my job."

Wassef Hamdi sat still while Doctor Frakowick suggested this might be a good time to call a break. Wassef seconded the motion.

CHAPTER TEN—Why Would She?

Melina stated, "My father announced that while the reports on Frank's financial and real estate holdings paint a picture of solvency, other concerns troubled him. One of his concerns was the FBI report stating that Frank had been observed in frequent contact with organized crime figures.

"My father said, 'What is your relationship with these individuals, and why do they call you Crazy Frankie?'"

Frank stared off into space. The question of how Wassef Hamdi had been able to access FBI reports gave Frank pause. Coming down to earth Frank thought, *You wouldn't have known that if you didn't have juice with the FBI.* What he said was, "Wiseguys use the term 'Crazy' as a term of respect. It means they see me as fearless and they respect that."

Wassef nodded.

Frank asked himself, *Why would Wassef Hamdi respect my willingness to live dangerously? Is Wassef also a man who lives dangerously? I think so.* "Night before last I played poker with those guys, had a drink with them and went home."

"How much do you drink?"

"Both my parents are alcoholic and frankly, that frightens me. There is no alcohol in my home. With Wiseguys, when it's politically expedient, I have a drink with them. I never have more than three drinks and only then over a long period of time."

Wassef said, "What if they insist you drink with them?"

"Only happened once. A Wiseguy named Rusty felt insulted about my unwillingness to have a third drink. I said: 'Rusty, my mother lives on a barstool, we don't even talk to each other, and my father's doing thirty to life because he couldn't get off the sauce. I damn sure don't want that for me!'

"If the day ever comes when I feel I really need another drink, I will have already had the last drink I will ever take. Usually those I drink with are mob guys. Mob guys are street guys. I'm strictly legal, but otherwise we're not all that different."

"So you admit it." Wassef said, "What is your religion?"

"I read the Qur'an when I was about fourteen. At other times I've read from the Old and the New Testament. The Book of Mormon is about the poorest written book I ever came across and I just couldn't get into it. I remain a skeptic and lack that sense of comfort you and your daughter derive from surrender to your religion. For me religion is academic while for you, religion is a matter of faith. I can't comment on whether my lack of faith is genetic or whether it's a product of upbringing; I don't have an answer to that question."

Wassef Hamdi continued, "Is there anything that would allow you to believe?"

Looking over their heads in reminiscence, Frank said, "To me, the body of a beautiful woman is the wonder of all wonders and how this wonder came about might lead one to suspect that if there is a God—she must be female."

Wassef's eyebrows shot up, while Doctor Frakowick put his hand over his mouth to hide his grin.

Frank continued, "If I have children, I can say for sure—if religion will work for them, then go for it—and don't waste time looking to me for spiritual guidance."

Wassef was grinning while at the same time shaking his head. He said, "I fail to understand . . . could you explain to me why my daughter should involve herself with you, even marry you?"

"I'm reminded of the axiom that every man marries his mother. In my case, in my early years, I was raised by my grandmother—a frail but strong-willed woman who was protective of those she loved.

"Mister Hamdi, unlike me, you have an unmarked face and

a gentle expression. But I suspect you are a dangerous man, more dangerous than me."

This, having been put out there, the table sat frozen and still. Wassef Hamdi relaxed the tension with a brief nod acknowledging Frank's perception.

Melina said, "Through all of this my stillness apparently weighed on father. He looked to me in such a way that—for the first time—invited my participation. My father asked if anyone had other questions and I gave a shake of my head to indicate no. Father then asked Frank if he would be willing to submit to a psychiatric evaluation by Doctor Frakowick. Grimacing, and then leaning back in his chair, hands on the edge of the table, Frank looked up at the ceiling, let out his breath and said, "When I learned Frakowick was a psychiatrist" . . . again shaking his head, "I saw this coming . . . but why? What's this all about?"

Wassef Hamdi said, "You will know in a few days, or you will never know."

Doctor Frakowick said, "Frank, I'll give you a call after I've had a chance to confer with Doctor Hamdi and Mr. Hamdi. At that time we can set up an appointment to do an evaluation."

Barney Kellett tried again. He said, "I've set up a Lie Detector appointment for you at the Police Station at 4 PM today. I suggest you keep that appointment."

They all stared at Barney Kellett. After a pause Frank said, "At 4 PM I'm going to be looking at a real estate deal. You made the appointment, you cancel it."

The eyes of Dr. Frakowick and Mr. Hamdi locked. The unspoken question hung in the air between them. *How in the world had Barney Kellett ever come to be the head of his own Detective Agency?*

"My father called the meeting to a close, thanked Frank for his cooperation, and noted that Frank had provided him with much to consider."

• • •

Annette said, "Melina, I've been watching your eyes. Whenever you speak of Frank standing tall, not being intimidated, being a strong man, your face and your eyes glow."

Melina nodded. "I needed to know if Frank truly is a strong man. Doctor Hussaini is Muslim, tall, handsome, rich, not athletic like Frank, and not strong like Frank or my father. He is courting me and would need my submission to bolster his ego. That neediness is something I do not find attractive. Also, I am hesitant to have him raise my child after I am gone. I came here today questioning whether the two of you were weak women, easily controlled, and so maybe Frank isn't as strong as he appears. Instead, I find two strong women who, by choice, have sublimated their will to Frank's. One might find this attractive."

Natalie nodded, saying, "You could give yourself to Frank but not to Dr. Hussaini."

Annette pointed her finger like a pistol at Melina, made a clicking sound and said, "Gotcha!"

• • •

At the women's next meeting Melina said, "Frank Grady is not apologetic about coming from the streets. I am from a foreign land, a rich family, am a Doctor, and have an aristocratic background." She laughed, "What a grand mix that would be." Then Melina paused . . . "In three words, how would you describe Frank?"

Natalie blinked. Then Annette smiled and said, "Tough, smart, limited."

CHAPTER ELEVEN—The Meeting

Wassef Hamdi pored over Dr. Frakowick's report, then called the house and requested an audience with Annette and Natalie.

Thinking on it, Annette said, "Natalie gets home in about 90 minutes . . . Frank will get home about six so now would be a good time for you to get here. It would allow you to spend time with each of us before Frank gets home."

· · ·

Mister Wassef Hamdi arrived and Annette greeted him at the door. She said, "Frank never misses in his judgment of character. Definitely, he told us, you're someone to be reckoned with."

With Wassef in tow Annette reentered the kitchen and her fingers flew while she chopped vegetables. Wassef said, "Why did you agree to have Natalie join with you and Frank?"

Annette thought on it. "Frank had been deserted by both his parents and then he lost both grandparents. He was alone by the time he was fifteen. My father deserted my mother and me while both of Natalie's parents, emotionally, had never been there for her. You could say the three of us together are healing each other."

"How would my daughter fit in all this?"

"Who else could she marry? As Frank pointed out, underneath your genteel appearance you are a tough and dangerous man. Frank is very protective of the two of us and would be protective of Melina as well. Immediately, Melina recognized this in Frank and the fact that he would not hesitate to take on a third woman does not detract from the toughness of this man; Frank would be there for us."

Wassef took a liking to the petite and gritty creature that is Annette. She was not intimidated by him and in response to his silent appraisal, Annette explained, "I'm a great cook, love it, and do most of the cooking. On a rare occasion Frank or Natalie will cook."

Surprised, Wassef said, "Frank cooks?"

Annette laughed. "Not often."

"I noticed a bookcase when I entered. May I take a look at it?"

"Go for it."

• • •

Wassef found a good selection of books on banking, psychoanalytic theory, psychology, and the only three decent books ever written on the subject of poker. There were a number of books on Civil War history and a small selection on World War Two. Four Shakespearean plays were at the end of the shelf along with a copy of Walt Whitman's Leaves of Grass.

When Wassef returned to the kitchen Annette said, "Did you find what you were looking for?"

"There was a book of handwritten notes."

"Frank's book of Tells," Annette said, "Each time Frank reads some clue or mannerism that tells him what the other player has or doesn't have, if it's not one he's familiar with. He writes it down in his Book of Tells."

Wassef nodded. "Very wise, painstaking and thorough."

"The section on banking belongs to Natalie. The rest are Frank's domain. Natalie and I like your daughter, admire her courage and while the three of us are very different we would be supportive of each other during Frank's absence and Melina's final illness."

Wassef nodding, said, "Who takes care of the housekeeping?"

"At the moment we do most of it. Frank loves rich carpeting and he's obsessive about running the vacuum cleaner. Natalie takes care of the house laundry and I'm in charge of the kitchen and the grocery shopping. We have a cleaning woman coming in twice a week and have a landscaper taking care of the yard. I was the first to join with Frank. We were on vacation when we met Natalie who was in a bad situation. When we left Natalie came with us. At the time there was no expectation that this would lead to a permanent relationship, but then it did. Seemed like the thing to do. I chose my life with Frank, Natalie made the same choice, and we have no regrets."

"No coercion? No manipulation?"

"None. Frank has a weird kind of intelligence, sees right through people and makes this work. It's because of Frank that I'm on my way to becoming a Master Chef. Without Frank I'd still be an oyster shucker or fruit picker living in poverty. Without permission from her parents, Natalie couldn't wipe her own ass. Now she stands up for herself, is a demon athlete, works in banking, and one day soon, she'll be going to college and playing basketball."

• • •

They heard the sound of the garage door going up. Natalie entered through the door just off from the kitchen. Even having been forewarned, Wassef was startled seeing that Natalie was such an Amazon of a woman. She was six feet tall in her bare feet, was dressed in a well-tailored dark blue business suit and with three inch high heels that showed off a great pair of legs.

Natalie said, "You must be Mister Wassef Hamdi."

Wassef admitted, "I am. I want to apologize. The two of you should have been invited to sit in on the meeting at Kellett Investigations. While in an Eastern society your attendance would have been inappropriate—this is a Western society—and my failure to offer you the opportunity to attend is inexcusable and for that I must apologize."

Annette said, "And now I need the two of you to get out of my kitchen."

• • •

In the yard, Natalie stooped to pick up a wad of paper that had blown in before she took a seat under the shade tree. "I have to say that Annette and I are feeling optimistic about a second meeting with Melina; we accept that Melina may not have a long life but still, this could work since both Annette and I agree, we like Melina and we like children."

Nodding, Wassef said, "My daughter echoed similar sentiments."

Previously charmed by the sparkle of Annette, Wassef recognized Natalie's innate intelligence, commanding appearance and assured persona. He thought, *along with a solid education, if she chose, Natalie Fisk might go far in the banking or corporate world.*

• • •

Frank entered the house, exited into the back yard, and shook Wassef's hand. Both men took seats, Natalie departed, and Wassef said, "In eastern societies, while men are supposedly dominant, many hunger to obey and at the directive of their spiritual leader will sacrifice themselves as human bombs. Women are to assume a role of submission to men, and like my wife, most are comfortable with this, while others, like my sister, cannot tolerate this and choose suicide as the way out."

• • •

"I spend," Frank said, "less time at the gaming table than I used to, which is good since all indications are that I'll be living with three women. Natalie wants to go to college and Melina may need to relocate to practice medicine."

• • •

Wassef called his wife. "Alsana, I have met with the two women, I have met with the man, I think you will like them, I like them, they are intelligent and stable, and the three women like each other. I think we can relax."

CHAPTER TWELVE—Melina Takes the Plunge

Meeting with Doctor Frakowick, Frank said, "Doc, the three women together are giving me orders. I still hit the casinos one or two nights a week but look forward to cutting back. Last night a big game kept me out later than expected. When I arrived home the three women were sitting in the dark waiting for me. My eyes were tired and I took a seat in the dark. In a beam of light I saw that Melina had taken off her shoes."

Melina said, "It's late. I have the morning shift so I'll be staying in your spare bedroom. I've picked out one of the quieter and smaller Hotels on the beach in Mazatlan and reserved rooms for 30 days. I chose a modest hotel since others staying there will be of modest means."

"So you want me," Frank said, "to take the three of you to Mazatlan for a 30 day trial-and-error vacation."

"I do. Then, if all goes well, I may agree to join with the three of you. If I join with you, usually, I will defer to you as the man of the house—but not always. This is essentially a test."

Annette giggled, "Frank, I can feel the heat from here. Your face is burning."

"How she knew I don't understand, but she was right."

"Hopefully," Melina said, "I will come to an understanding, within those 30 days, as to whether a marriage with you is something that will work for me, and each of you will learn whether a life with the three of us and our children is something you want."

• • •

They landed in Mazatlan and a dusty and ancient limousine transported them past the large and upscale north beach hotels to their modest hotel on the southern end of the beach. Red tiled flooring in the lobby, rambunctious scarlet bougainvillea plants and butterflies in the Courtyard, soft frothy waves lapping on the beach, and a sky of clear blue with feathery wisps of clouds—all were working their magic. This modest economy class hotel was lean but comfortable and the temperature was perfect.

Melina and Frank's room on the second floor had a balcony that looked out on the water. They watched as Annette and Natalie ran into the soft lapping waves and swam out some distance. Melina said, "They're strong swimmers."

Annette and Natalie had persuaded Melina to purchase a Bikini, she changed in the bathroom, and when she came out Frank could not help but marvel at the delicate grace of the woman. He said, "God you look good! Turn around so I can see you from the back!"

Melina made a slow and self-conscious turn. With olive skin flushed, she said, "In the Muslim world I would not dare being seen in this swim suit."

• • •

Melina was unsure of herself in open water. She chose the small kidney-shaped hotel pool. It was surrounded by palm trees and potted plants in full flower. A fountain was splashing water into the green and blue tiled pool. The water felt sensual and they each swam a few strokes, but somehow, Melina's butt or hip kept bumping up against Frank.

They left the pool holding hands. When they entered their room Melina melted into his arms. She may have been a conservative Muslim, but sexually, she was not the least bit conservative and knowing that her time was limited, now abandoning virginity, she also abandoned inhibition.

• • •

The restaurant had vivid Mexican décor with fat paper flowers, International flags, piñatas, and local Mexican musicians serenaded the table with gusto. As musicians they were enthusiastic, more so than talented, and Frank concluded that, *mostly, what they are is needy.* Frank provided a generous tip.

• • •

In the middle of the night, sheet lightning filled the sky to the South. The night was warm and not raining and Melina and Frank arose and went out on the balcony to watch. Frank held Melina cradled in his arms while on another balcony they saw Annette being held by Natalie. The moment was magical.

• • •

The next day the four of them, with mild sun and windburn after a four hour pleasure cruise, entered the hotel restaurant. They had taken the only unoccupied table when, from the kitchen, there was a cry of pain along with the sound of something breaking. Melina marched into the kitchen saying, "I am a doctor."

A waiter arrived at Frank's table saying, "The doctor requests that you go for her medical bag."

Frank arrived with Melina's medical kit. She gave the man shots of Novocaine and stitched up the nasty cut across the heel of the young man's hand. Also, she provided him with an antibiotic. Annette, with raised eyebrows, looked questioningly to Frank. He said, "Go." And Annette rushed into the shorthanded kitchen.

• • •

Frank watched as the three women entered the sea waters. Frank took to the water as an ordeal to overcome, swam out far enough that it tired him and cooled him off. Swimming back, he poured himself into a chair under a beach umbrella while watching the women cavorting in the water. The sight of this filled him with a peace that was sublime.

• • •

Frank followed as the three women toured the various shops

situated on the beach road, then toured the large market in the center of town. Everything delighted the women. Attracted to the scents, sounds, brightly colored clothing, and varieties of silver and turquoise jewelry, they grazed and gathered.

Some evenings they explored the various forms of entertainment. The music was played with musical instruments not familiar to their ears, and sometimes with only a modicum of talent, but it was always lively and entertaining.

The four of them fell into a relaxed groove. Melina said, "Life with the three of you, this could work for me."

• • •

Melina was scheduled for an interview at Farwest Children's Hospital in Seattle.

At breakfast, Melina said, "I took my medical training at the University of Washington, served my Internship in Las Vegas, and despite growing up in a dry land, or perhaps because of it, the Seattle rains didn't bother me like they did the others. Sometimes I sat for hours just watching and listening to the rain."

"If we move to Seattle," Melina said, "and if the position at Farwest does not come through, there is a moderate and liberal Muslim community in Seattle and I am prepared to then open a private practice."

Natalie said, "With a move to Seattle I could enter the University of Washington's Economics Program. Also, their woman's basketball program is very good."

They all looked at Annette. She said, "Chefs are in demand everywhere so a move to Seattle would be fine with me."

"I grew up," Frank said, "in Tacoma, thirty miles to the south of Seattle. I could always fly back to Las Vegas if I wanted bigger action at the tables but I wouldn't miss Vegas."

• • •

The decision to move to Seattle was a slam dunk. The women flew back to Las Vegas while Frank booked a flight to Seattle. On arrival he booked a room in the Olympic Hotel and began a tour of properties for sale on the shores of Lake Washington.

The waterfront property he found on Mercer Island had its own dock, was less than a mile from the Lake Washington Bridge, had an air of privacy and a broad weeping-willow tree in the middle of a large lawn that sloped down to the water's edge.

Frank called Las Vegas and reported, "As Boeing Aircraft goes— so goes the Seattle real estate market. At this time the market is low and it's a good time to buy. Some wit even posted a sign, saying, 'The last one to leave Seattle please turn off the lights.'"

• • •

The house was large and modern. Annette was gratified to learn it had a four-burner gas range, a grill and two ovens. "The house," Frank said, "is eighteen years old, cheerful and roomy with lots of windows. There are four bedrooms, two and a half bathrooms, a three-car garage, an outside deck on the lake side of the house— plus a dock on the lake. The property lines are marked on two sides by walls of flowering rhododendrons against five feet high wooden fences. The lake forms the boundary at the back while the street forms the boundary to the front."

• • •

In tandem, Annette and Natalie drove the Rolls Royce and the Mercedes to Seattle. Then Frank had new carpeting, furniture and household goods moved into the house and the three of them took up residence. They called Melina every day.

CHAPTER THIRTEEN—Barney Kellett

Wassef Hamdi, along with his wife Alsana, a slender and well-preserved beauty, arrived by taxi from Sea Tac Airport. Melina's mother looked closely at Frank, then broke into a smile and shook his hand. Turning to her husband, she said, "Leave me with the women."

"Wassef and Frank stood on the lawn while the women explored the property, then marched into the house. Wassef and Frank strolled towards the Lake.

Taking seats on the dock, Wassef said, "My wife, she's never shook a man's hand before."

"You and your wife," Frank said, "are Muslim and yet you approve of me as a son-in-law. This must be hard for you?"

"It is. But you have the redeeming feature of being without pretense. It has been our experience that sometimes a Muslim man courting a Muslim woman will present himself as a considerate man only to become, after the marriage ceremony, a ruthless, even brutal, tyrant. Sometimes the bride will choose suicide as the only way out.

Frank looked at Wassef, but didn't ask.

Wassef continued, "Yes, that is what happened to my sister. That is why my wife and I accepted that life in a western country, for our daughter, would be acceptable. You are an articulate man who makes no effort to conceal who and what you are. My daughter, like my sister, is unusually bright and unsuited to be any man's doormat.

And for this reason I had encouraged my daughter to enter medical school. A female physician would register prestige and authority even in some Muslim communities.

"My daughter insisted I would have to meet you in person before my disapproval would influence her decision. It was outrageous that a Muslim woman would defy her father like that, and yet, it proved to be the right thing for her to do."

A flock of Canadian geese were busy crapping on the far end of Frank's dock. He let them be and said, "I'll scrub the dock tomorrow. I suspect that Melina will usually go along with what I say but when she disagree's I suspect she will also let me know."

"She will. The report we received from Barney Kellett on the content of your character frightened my wife and I—we feared for our daughter. Yet the tape of your meeting with Barney Kellett demonstrated your willingness to protect Annette and Natalie. Barney had ordered that tape destroyed. Instead, Chuck Rose played the tape for me and my wife. Mister Rose does not like Mister Kellett.

"Again, at the meeting at Kellett Investigations, when you expressed your outrage that Annette and Natalie had been excluded from the meeting, again I saw your passion and my opinion of you reached a turning point. You made it clear that you will not allow the interests of Annette and Natalie to be set aside."

"Since you are protective of Annette and Natalie, I suspect you would also protect my daughter. However, on the day my daughter decides she wants out, you will let go or you will have to deal with me—and, as you recognized, I can be dangerous."

"Plus," Frank said, "you somehow have access to FBI files. I suspect your sister's husband met with some unpleasantness."

"That he did."

• • •

Melina was interviewed for a position at Farwest Children's Hospital. She returned to the Lake Washington home in a state of unease, seated herself in the living room and reported, "Dr. Rivers said he was impressed with my Letters of Recommendation and with my interview. He said, 'I usually consult with the Board before making a final decision, but with your character and medical qualifications, in this instance, the Board process will be bypassed. Your duties begin at 6 AM on Monday. Welcome aboard."'

Frank said, "You look uneasy."

She nodded and said, "Something about Doctor Rivers doesn't feel right."

"Melina, you're a beautiful woman in a foreign land, and at present you appear to be alone and vulnerable. Doctor Rivers could be anticipating something more from you. If you do take the job, when he realizes you're not alone, he may back off, but if he doesn't, well then, we'll have to deal with this."

• • •

Doctor Rivers then received a visit from Barney Kellett who presented his business card and said, "Kellett Investigations is a Las Vegas firm and we had been hired by the father of a local physician who, belatedly, became concerned that his daughter was being groomed to become the third woman in the stable of a pervert. Our investigation prompted the four of them to flee Las Vegas and relocate in Seattle."

Doctor Rivers stated, "I take it you're referring to Dr. Melina Hamdi." Doctor Rivers then arose from his chair saying, "I thank you for your concerns Sir. This is a matter that can and will be rectified."

Doctor Rivers called the Ward and ordered Dr. Hamdi to report to his office. When Melina reported, Dr. Rivers said, "You misled me! You neglected to inform me you were involved in an illicit relationship. Pack up your things and get out of this hospital. You're through!"

After this righteous sounding outburst, Melina put two and two together and said, "Barney Kellett! Coming off the elevator I thought the man leaving through the front entrance looked familiar. He had a jaunty step and seemed quite pleased with himself."

Melina then drew herself to her full height, put one foot forward, and softly through clenched teeth stated, "I'm leaving but I'll be coming back with my father and the man I intend to marry. You have no clue who you will be dealing with. For this insult, we are going to turn you and this hospital upside down! Be prepared for the worst . . . because it is definitely coming!"

Going to her office Melina reached Frank by phone and reported, "I need you Frank, so don't you leave! I'll be right over!"

• • •

Frank was in the yard when Melina's car came blazing down the driveway and to a screeching halt. Melina climbed out of the car and announced—"Frank, you're going to marry me and I'm giving up the apartment and coming to live with the three of you. The tears came as she continued, "I want you and my father to get together and tear Barney Kellett and Dr. Rivers new assholes."

Then, wiping away her tears and calmer, Melina said, "Where's the phone? I need to speak with my father."

They listened long enough to learn that Barney Kellett had been to see Dr. Rivers who then fired Melina, then Frank, Annette, and Natalie retreated outside, while Melina continued venting, now in Arabic, to her father.

Melina came out of the house saying, "Frank, father says don't you do anything until he gets here. He and mother will be on the next available flight!" Then she charged back to the phone.

Shaking his head, Frank muttered, "Doctor Rivers doesn't have a clue, but Barney Kellett, how could he have been so dumb as to unlock that cage door?"

• • •

Wassef and Alsana Hamdi's flight arrived at Sea Tac Airport and Melina and Frank met them at the Off-Loading Gate. Their luggage was collected and Frank drove. The mood was somber, no one spoke while Melina sat in back holding her mother's hand.

The women entered the house.

"Let us," Wassef said, "take a walk down to your dock. Interesting, when disaster struck, my daughter reached out to you before me. That tells me of her commitment to you and you to her. Also she needs the cover of a Marriage Certificate to become a Naturalized American Citizen."

"What," Frank said, "about Barney Kellett?"

"Your responsibility is to protect my daughter, to remove her from harm's way. Now, as the first step in setting the stage for an upcoming lawsuit, I would encourage an orderly haste into marriage and you will then remove my daughter from the scene of the crime."

Frank skipped a rock along the surface of the lake. "I think Melina would like to be married in a Mosque."

"There are difficulties, you being an infidel, but you being willing to be married in a Mosque, I will overcome those difficulties."

• • •

Frank was to learn that Wassef visited the Imam and quietly read off the names and addresses of each and every one of the Imam's many relatives still living in the Middle East. Terrified, the Imam quickly agreed to marry Melina and Frank in the Mosque.

Wassef has a nice smile—but his teeth are made of steel.

Frank and Melina were married in the Seattle Mosque she had attended while taking her medical training. The ceremony was conducted with dignity and brevity by a sweating Imam.

• • •

Lake Union is an unpretentious small body of water attached to the canal that connects Lake Washington, through the Ballard Locks, to the Puget Sound.

Frank and Melina were gathered up and taken to Lake Union and loaded aboard an amphibious plane. Melina and her mother were conversing in Arabic while a grinning Wassef said, "Frank, taking in my daughter while in this monogamous land, you are a brave man." Then, while saying goodbye to his daughter, he slipped an envelope into Frank's hand saying, "This is my daughters dowry, also a small token of my esteem. You and my daughter must remain in residence in Canada for at least three weeks."

Melina and Frank were being flown to Lake Louise. They were airborne and settled down when Frank opened the envelope. His father-in-law had given Frank a check for $10,000.

• • •

The hotel on Lake Louise was serene and elegant. Dining with other couples was pleasant, as were the solitary walks on the trails around Lake Louise. They would have liked to stay longer but there was much to do.

• • •

They learned, on their return, that an arson fire had destroyed the Las Vegas offices of Kellett Investigations. Insurance Investigators found an empty gas can in the trash barrel behind Barney's home. To avoid prosecution, Barney Kellett withdrew his insurance claim.

• • •

While Frank and Melina were on their honeymoon, bookcases had been built along the length of the upstairs hall, the kitchen had received an overhaul, and the house was ready for their return.

• • •

Melina received a call from Mr. Charles Fry, a prominent Seattle attorney who was also the President of the Board for Farwest Children's Hospital. Farwest had been notified that a lawsuit was pending for Termination Without Due Process. Attorney Fry asked if they could meet informally for a preliminary and off-the-record discussion."

Melina said solemnly, "Perhaps you might discuss this with my husband." With a twinkle in her eye, Melina handed the phone over to Frank. He listened, then asked Attorney Fry, "By chance are you a married man?"

He replied, "Very much so."

"Perhaps you and your wife would come to our home for dinner at say, 6 PM tomorrow?"

Mr. and Mrs. Fry accepted the invitation.

• • •

Housekeepers and landscapers had been brought in and the house and yard were immaculate. On Charles and Jenny Fry's arrival, the meeting and shaking of hands was cordial. The women then gathered in the house while Frank was showing Charles the rest of the property. Out of the blue, Charles Fry said, "When I talked with Chuck Rose I learned that Dr. Frakowick did a Psychological

Examination and Profile on you, and that neither he nor Barney Kellett have had access to its contents."

"Chuck's OK." Shaking his head he continued, "But Barney Kellett . . . well, Barney Kellett, he's something else. I have a copy of that evaluation and I'm willing to show it to you. It goes on for four pages and boils down to the fact that when I was a boy my only source of support came from my grandparents. Grandmother died first. When Grandfather died I was then a boy all alone. That triggered a lot of pain. Years later I joined the Navy, and the Navy became my new family but then a crazy Lieutenant JG, got it in his head that I must be a 'sleeper' planted in the USN by some foreign entity. I didn't know then whether to laugh or cry.

• • •

Entering the basement, Charles looked at the exercise equipment. In response to his questioning look Frank said, "Most days I do fifteen minutes on the abdominal machine, fifteen minutes on the rowing machine, and fifteen minutes on the heavy bag. Other days I do more. Sometimes I work on the speed bag for as much as fifteen minutes. I should be working less on the heavy bag and more on the speed bag but I like the feel of hitting something solid."

Charles Fry nodded, said, "Now that does not surprise me."

"When I was in Las Vegas I worked out with pro boxers twice a week. But at present I've lost the desire."

Charles nodded. "So much is going on, you needing to be responsive to three women."

"That too."

• • •

Dinner was called. It began with Court Bouillon, sole, then lamb and ended with a salad in the European style. For desert they had peach cobbler. During dinner Charles Fry said to Melina, "I hesitate to ask—but how did you come to know Frank?"

"I heard tales about Frank and his living with two women. My staring at him got his attention. He saw me seeing him. Then, in the cafeteria, this same well-dressed man with the bumpy nose and scarred face sat down across from me with two packets of food. He opened both packets and I saw and smelled seasoned gourmet Middle Eastern foods. He began eating from one packet and pushed the other packet over to me. I tried the food; well—I think you might say that was the beginning."

Charles then looked over at Frank who said, "I was visiting my tax consultant after his gall bladder surgery when for first time I saw this gorgeous creature in hospital scrubs coming out of his room. She stared at me. Max, my tax consultant, told me that she had nothing to do with his gall bladder, was a pediatrician, was asking questions about me and the two women living with me. I turned and followed her to the cafeteria and recognized her disinterest in cafeteria food. Making inquiries, I learned Dr. Hamdi was from Egypt and the next day I arrived with gourmet Middle Eastern foods and it was no contest; cafeteria food was embarrassed to sit at the same table with Kasum's Indian Cuisine."

. . .

Charles Fry and Frank took seats on the dock while the women retired to the house deck. Without preamble Charles said, "I assume there will be no others?"

"There will not."

"We would like this case to go away. With my recommendation I think the Board will be persuaded to provide a modest settlement along with Dr. Hamdi's reinstatement."

"What about Dr. Rivers?"

"Ah yes! Dr. Rivers. . . . His days at Farwest are numbered. When I took over as President of the Board I inherited both Dr. Rivers and his supporters. There have been earlier rumblings, and even before this incident his support was eroding . . . has now eroded. Dr. Rivers, by example, had promoted a predatory sexual climate at Farwest—but the cauldron is now coming to a boil. Two of Dr. Rivers crony's, hearing the rumbling of storm clouds on the horizon—have already handed in their resignations."

. . .

The final say as to whether Melina would settle out of Court was hers. Melina said, "Let your attorneys draft an agreement with a settlement package and then we will see."

Melina was offered reinstatement plus an out of Court Settlement. She kept them waiting for 24 hours before accepting. "My wife" Frank said, "so genteel, is also one tough cooky."

CHAPTER FOURTEEN—Children

Annette said, "Frank . . . take a seat."

He did. Frank noted a cheerful and conspiratorial air about the women. He thought, *they're up to something.*

Annette stood before him and said, "Frank, I'm pregnant. You're about to become a father."

He felt dizzy. The women had kept him busy enough, without immediate results, and so there had been concerns. Those concerns, now put to rest, led them to cancel Frank's visit to the Fertility Clinic.

• • •

Frank experienced a vague sense of anxiety. He told Melina, "I don't get it. I'm having dreams of death and murder."

Melina called Doctor Frakowick.

Doc Frakowick replied, "Uh huh—I'm glad you called. Now let me speak with Frank."

Frank said, "Doc, I hate to admit it, but I'm terrified that Annette might die or that once Annette has her child she will lose interest in me. And my dreams . . . they're scary and they don't make any sense."

"Relax Frank—you're reliving the trauma of your childhood— expectant fathers, men like you who have experienced traumatic childhood losses or rejections, may become fearful that once the child is born they will once again be rejected. The number one cause of death in pregnant women is murder by the expectant father."

"Wha-at! They'd have to be crazy!" Then, with a sigh, Frank said, "Thanks Doc. Sweet Jesus God! I suppose it makes sense. Now I understand. Okay . . .. Don't worry. No harm will come to Annette or our baby."

Frank's dreams changed

. . .

Melina said, "Frank, wake up. Annette's having contractions."

Having rehearsed this moment, they were prepared and efficient. Annette was placed in the back seat with Melina while Natalie was in the front seat and Frank drove. They arrived at the Hospital Emergency Entrance at 3 AM and were met by two nurses with a rolling gurney.

Melina said to the Nurse on the desk, "I'm Dr. Hamdi. My husband is the father so when he's finished parking the car please direct him to the Delivery room."

Frank entered the ER. He headed for the delivery room while Natalie dealt with the nurse who was attempting to determine whether Annette's pregnancy was a consequence of sexual abuse. Natalie laughed and said, "We make some pretty stringent demands on Frank but I wouldn't call it abuse. He does seem to like it."

The nurse tried again saying, "Still, if this is an unwanted pregnancy . . .."

Natalie said, "Uh-unh. Annette asked Frank to give her a baby and he has. I've also asked him to father me a child."

At that moment Annette's mother, along with Frank's father, who was now out of prison and on Parole, burst through the Emergency entrance. Marguerite said, "Where's my daughter?"

Natalie and Marguerite headed for the Delivery Room.

The nurse shook her head in surrender.

. . .

Annette's baby was placed in her arms—then she reached out one hand to Frank.

Their son was named Cody, and last name Tyler. Their beautiful son provided a demonstration of great lungs, and having thus asserted himself, promptly went to sleep.

Frank said, "Being a father . . . what a grand feeling."

Melina noted that Cody was a healthy and well put together little guy.

• • •

Frank received word of his mother's death. She had used the fact of her husband's incarceration, along with her own emphysema, to qualify for Welfare checks all these years The only attachment she ever maintained was her parasitic hold on the butt of the Welfare Department. Her ashes were assigned to Elliot Bay, not far from where she grew up . . .

It was over.

• • •

Annette said, "Frank, wake up. Natalie's having contractions." Having rehearsed this moment, they were prepared, efficient, and Natalie was placed in the back seat with Melina while Frank drove. They arrived at the Hospital Emergency Entrance at 1 AM and were met by two nurses with a rolling gurney.

Frank parked the car, entered the ER, and headed for the Delivery Room.

• • •

Natalie, with little prompting or difficulty, delivered up a large child she named John. He would grow to be a large and athletically gifted boy. Others sometimes refer to Frank as Franky, but as John grew, no one ever referred to John as Johnny. Frank often wondered, *how does he do that?*

• • •

Six months after David Grady got out of prison, like two old barnacles, Frank and his father were sitting in lawn chairs out on the dock and fishing for whatever drifted by. What they usually caught were perch, sunfish, and sometimes a smallmouth bass. They were catching nothing that day and it didn't matter. For David, after twenty-plus years in prison, the smells coming off lake Washington were intoxicating.

David said, "Frankie, on my being locked up, your Grandfather sent me the AA Big Book. Was that a reprimand or was it caring? I wasn't sure. I didn't read it at first but eventually I got into it. I'd done four years before I actually got serious about the program and started working the Steps. In Step One, I accepted I was powerless over alcohol and that my life had become unmanageable; that was too fucking obvious.

"The Second Step says: We came to believe a power greater than our selves could restore us to sanity. That was a tough step for me. I was in prison where I was a well-respected con. I took pride in being a pretty smart guy. Then one day it dawned on me that if I'm so damn smart *then what the hell am I doing in prison?* It came to me that my thinking and behavior, all of it, was really nuts.

"Then I came to the Third Step. It said: We made a decision to turn our will and our lives over to the care of God as we understood him."

"I struggled with that step for six months; used all my willpower to take that step and I couldn't do it. Then one day, while being let out to the yard, I looked up at the sky and it hit me. I dropped to my knees and with tears running down my face, I raised my hands and eyes up to the sky and shouted: *If you're not up there then I am screwed!* If that isn't surrender I don't know what is.

"Then Captain Cutter showed up I thought, *Oh Oh!* . . . Cutter was generally considered the toughest, meanest screw in the joint. Cutter said, 'Let's take a walk Grady.'"

"I thought for sure Cutter was going to put me in the hole. Then Cutter said, 'Grady, would it be okay with you if I were to pray for you tonight?'"

• • •

In the middle of the night, Melina's flight from the Mayo Clinic landed at Sea Tac Airport. A tired Melina came through the offloading gate and Frank wrapped her up in a hug. Their kiss was gentle.

On the drive home Frank said, "Good Conference?"

Melina nodded, "It was."

Exhausted, Melina took time to look in on babies Cody and John who were asleep. She touched the boy's faces and retreated. Frank served Melina an East Indian vegetable dish along with a good Kosher rye bread and a glass of whole milk. Relieved at being home, Melina ate as much as she could, which wasn't much, and had a soak in the tub before being toddled off to bed. She was asleep in an instant and still as a statue; she seemed barely to breathe. Frank leaned on his elbow and looked at the wonder he saw as Melina. There was a full moon shining through the window and Melina was bathed in moonlight. Frank thought, *she has no idea how precious, how beautiful she is.*

With the beginning of daylight, Melina sighed, took a deep breath, turned on her side and said, "Frank, hold me please."

Melina didn't need money and having a strong social conscience she now devoted her medical attention to the Free Clinic.

• • •

Melina said, "Frank, get me to the hospital."

Frank's father and Annette's mother were now a couple and stayed at the house to watch over the children while Frank burned up Highway 405.

Wassef and Alsana had traveled from Egypt to be present at the birth of their grandchild and David Grady put in the call to their hotel.

The delivery was difficult—took hours. An exhausted Melina had delivered a beautiful baby girl she named Alsana.

Little Alsana had the olive complexion and delicate beauty of her mother. She would grow into a reflective and sometimes stubborn child with occasional glimpses of evasive impishness.

Melina and baby returned home four days later.

• • •

There are advantages for children growing up in a multi-lingual household. When Melina said anything to the children in English she would repeat the same message in Arabic. In the same way, Marguerite and Annette would repeat in Spanish what they had said to the children in English. There was no direct pressure on the children to learn three languages, yet each of them were acquiring three languages along with other life skills.

CHAPTER FIFTEEN— The Inquisition

Alvin Frugate Jr., one of Frank's boyhood classmates, had chosen J. Edger Hoover as his role-model. Alvin entered the FBI with a law degree and an encyclopedic knowledge of governmental and organizational dynamics and was moved into a controllable administrative function.

FBI Director Alan Buechner said, "Frugate, you have a talent for pointing out what needs being done. Others then volunteer for the undertaking. You are sliding up the ladder of success on the work of others—and that creeps me out."

Frugate said, "Doesn't matter. You'll be gone by the end of the month and I'll still be sliding up the ladder of success."

Director Buechner warned others about Frugate but nobody listened. Frugate was rising on the crest of the volunteer's success and when the volunteer failed, it was the volunteer who sank.

The word was, "Frugate knows how to delegate."

Truth is—Alvin seldom delegated. Others volunteered; took care of Alvin. Everyone did. Without ever having worked a case, made an arrest, or worked up a sweat, Alvin Frugate floated up the ladder of command to the position of FBI Director.

• • •

Cherry trees were in blossom along the Potomac when Agent

Tom Nichols reported to Director Frugate's Office. "I'll get right to the point," Frugate said, "Years ago, Adele Yonkey, a former classmate of mine, was murdered. The investigation turned up no suspects. Recently, an anonymous phone caller stated he thought he saw Adele Yonkey get in a car with Frank Grady the day before she disappeared; he had assumed he was mistaken because Frank Grady was stationed at the San Diego Naval Station at the time. The caller had recently learned that Frank Grady could have flown in, murdered Adele, then flown back to San Diego on that long weekend when Adele disappeared.

"As a boy," Director Frugate said, "Adele Yonkey had rejected Frank Grady, and I had a premonition then that one day he was going to kill her. Agent Nichols, you did an excellent job on your last case. I know you're tired, but you're the best we have. So, if you're willing, I'll have you posted to Seattle to take charge of the Adele Yonkey case."

"Yes Sir, I'll get right on it."

• • •

To Agent Nichols it seemed that the National Interest is the same as the Bureau's Interest, and therefore the Director is Infallible.

"Agent Nichols," Director Frugate said, "let your family know that once you've wrapped up this case, and having a good idea who it is, that may not take long, then you will receive thirty days of convalescent leave. Wrap this up and then you and your family can take a long and well-earned vacation."

Emotionally exhausted, and in failing health, Nichols soldiered on.

• • •

Agent Kimberly Wheaten was assigned as Second in Command in the Yonkey case. Her manner and wardrobe reflected she was all business, was ambitious, and dismissive of her own slender beauty.

Agent Dennis Huff reported to Agent Wheaten for duty.

"Agent Huff," Agent Wheaten said, "I'm the Primary Investigator in this case and you've been assigned as my Second. You are a retired Marine Officer and were assigned to NCIS late in your career and you never rose above the rank of Lieutenant. How come?"

"I was an 18 year old with an eighth grade education when I joined the Marines. Years later, I received a battlefield commission. When I was transferred to NCIS, as a Lieutenant, I found myself too much behind a desk. I belong on the ground and not riding a desk. I put in my twenty, reverted back to First Sergeant, took my retirement as an enlisted man, and then signed up with the FBI. What I don't get is, I'm new to the FBI, and this is a high-profile case, so why have I landed in a high profile case?"

"Our prime suspect," Agent Wheaton said, "even unarmed, is a dangerous man. Quantico reports that you are as good, armed or unarmed, as anyone they've ever seen, that you're world class in firearms and in judo. When and if we go to arrest this man, we may need more muscle or firepower than I personally can supply."

• • •

Huff and Wheaten went to interview Adele Yonkey's former roommate Cindy Fields. A neighbor said, "You'll probably find Cindy at the Jazz Dance Hall. She spends free time there."

As they were leaving, Dennis Huff remarked, "I like her already."

Agent Wheaten flashed her credentials on the bouncer and asked him to point out Cindy Fields. When they identified themselves, Cindy Fields curled her lip and headed for the dance floor. Huff followed and began to dance. He was a muscular, decent-looking guy with a shrapnel scarred face, and surprisingly graceful. He gave himself completely to the sound of jazz—was a wonder to behold, spinning, jumping in the air, doing splits, and feet flying in moves they'd never seen before. Couples stopped to watch. Grabbing Cindy's hand he had her laughing as he tossed her in the air and guided her through moves she never knew she had.

The interview with Cindy was cordial, but provided them with nothing new. Agent Wheaten was thanking her when Dennis grabbed Cindy's hand and led her back on the floor for one last dance. Together, they tore up the floor.

On leaving, Dennis detected the hint of a smile on Agent Wheaten's face. She said, "You have any more surprises for me?"

Grinning, he said, "Maybe; maybe not."

• • •

The Puget Sound Naval Shipyard is perched on the edge of the Sound and is the sole sustenance for Bremerton, a town of mostly World War Two built small houses. Driving onto the Naval Base, Huff and Wheaten located the office of Base Commander Admiral Clay. He promised the Navy's full cooperation while directing them to USN Lieutenant Max Krautz.

Agents Huff and Wheaten introduced themselves. Lieutenant Krautz asked, "What can I do for you?"

"We're taking another look at the Adele Yonkey case."

Lieutenant Krautz took a deep breath. Gathering himself he said, "I remember the case. I was a junior officer attached to NCIS at the time. We were stalemated and the case went inactive. Reports stated that Adele was a quiet, conservative, and dignified young woman who liked order, didn't like surprises, was good at her job, and got along with everyone. Her ex-husband was out of the country at the time and we found no evidence of other romantic involvements."

Agent Wheaten said, "Did the name Frank Grady ever come up?"

Krautz gave it some thought, and shook his head before saying, "Doesn't ring a bell."

Agent Wheaten showed a Navy photo of Frank Grady. "Do you recognize this man?"

The Lieutenant's eyes widened, "Damned right! But that was before the Adele Yonkey case. I was at the San Diego Naval Station when I entered the biggest-money poker game I ever saw in the Navy. He broke me, eventually broke the game."

• • •

FBI Agent Thomas Nichols was a tall, slender man with a gentle, aesthetic expression, but the first time Agent Dennis Huff saw Agent Nichols he thought, *this man is a burned-out wreck.*

Agent Kimberly Wheaten hesitated, then said, "Nichols seeks out the toughest assignments. He's a true company man."

Huff said, "Is he good?"

"He's good—tireless—or he was."

"Well what I'm seeing looks like shellshock."

• • •

Almost from the beginning the case was a disaster . . . Nichols had lost his perspective, and his sole focus was on a search for evidence pointing to Frank Grady.

They found nothing. Other than the one hearsay phone call from an anonymous caller—there was nothing. Agent Nichols said, "I have a hunch the evidence is here, right in front of our noses, and we're not seeing it."

• • •

Agents Wheaten and Huff interviewed Frank's former classmate Wayne Phillips. He was a personable and handsome man who said, "I went to commiserate with Frank when his dog was run over, and for that he knocked me down. Frank Grady's nothing but a thug, always has been, always will be."

Back then, Wayne had folded his arms and smirked, "You just lost your best friend." Frank knocked Wayne down, gathered up little Toby, and buried him in the lot behind where he lived.

• • •

The muscular, square-jawed and hard-nosed ex-Marine Officer, along with all-business FBI Agent Kimberly Wheaton, so different from each other, yet they were a nice fit. They reviewed the crime scene photos, and revisited the crime scene. The offender had evidently been familiar with the area, but their visit told them nothing more than that.

Agent Dennis Huff said, "Wheaten, Agent Nichols is a burned-out wreck."

She nodded, "I think the repeated exposure to the horrific cases he's worked have left a mark on his soul, if not on his face, has solidified his early religious training and his belief in the existence of the Devil. His pursuit of the offender has been maniacal. For sure he's lost a step or two."

"Well what I'm seeing looks like shellshock."

"Huff, we've had this conversation before."

"We have. And it's not going away."

CHAPTER SIXTEEN—The Deal

The wind was whipping up whitecaps as Frank drove across the Lake Washington Bridge. He noted he was being tailed by a blue Ford.

The houses hugging the western shore of Mercer Island had one or more large shade trees and shared a sense of privacy. Frank entered the house, took up his revolver, exited on the lake side of the house, and cut through his neighbor's lake-side yards. His pursuer had eased up to the curb two houses back, and had rolled down the window.

Melina and Annette met the minivan bringing the children home. Melina spoke to the driver, then to the children. The interior, initially quiet, rumbled, and then spewed forth three children. Cody and John each took one of little sister Alsana's hands and walked her into the house. Annette had lingered and stationed herself between the pursuer and the children. Something else—The driver that had tailed Frank became aware that Frank Grady was at his open window and with a revolver in his hand.

"You come up with a gun and you're dead! Who are you?"

"I'm FBI Agent White."

Frank examined White's credentials and handed them back. "Why were you following me?"

"I'm not authorized to discuss that at this time."

"Which is FBI-speak for you don't have a fucking clue." Then with a wave of his hand he beckoned Annette. When she arrived, Frank said, "He's FBI." He unloaded the revolver, handed it to her, passed in front of the Agent's car, and climbed into the passenger seat. "Okay Agent White, let's go talk to your boss."

• • •

Frank can be aggressive when he's playing for high-stakes . . . in poker or in other games.

It was raining again as they passed over the Lake Washington Bridge and Agent White asked, "Why are we going to the office of my boss?"

"I want to know what this is about. I'll be taking it from the top because you're low level and probably don't know squat."

• • •

The Federal Building's hallways were wide, the ceilings tall, freshly painted, and the floors were immaculate in what looked like grey granite. Steps echoed. Agent White, chin up and swallowing hard, walked down the hall to the Office of Agent Thomas Nichols.

When Agent White exited the office his downcast eyes told a tale. Frank then strode into Agent Nichols' inner sanctum.

Frank thought, *Nichols reminds me of the hull of that burned-out house I drove by yesterday.* He demanded, "Let's cut to the chase. You people already know everything there is to know about me so what's going on?"

• • •

Frank's former classmate Alvin Frugate, now FBI Director Frutgate, had opened a file on Frank Grady when Natalie joined up with Frank and Annette. When they moved to Las Vegas, the FBI had recorded Frank's contacts with Artie Karp and other wiseguys.

Agent Nichols walked over to the window and paused to look out over Third Avenue—not a pretty view. Turning and taking a deep breath, he stated, "We know you're legally married to Dr. Melina Hamdi who holds dual citizenship in this country as well as being a citizen of Egypt. We also know of your relationships with Annette Tyler and Natalie Fisk, and you have three young children living with you."

Frank read an unspoken insinuation in this last statement, and wide eyed, he said, "Nichols, you're reaching and that tells me that you're desperate. Why this desperate search for something linking me to Adele? You're searching for something, for anything . . . which indicates you have nothing. I knew an Adele Yonkey when I was in the sixth and seventh grades. We were neighbors . . . haven't seen her since we were kids."

"We know that Adele Yonkey came to you to make amends for the way she rejected you and then you killed her. We have a witness who saw Adele getting into your car on the day she disappeared. Now knowing where to look we will gather more corroborating evidence before we take you to Court."

Frank stared at Nichols. Then with a shake of his head he said, "Nichols, are you on some kind of hallucinogenic? This is Bullshit! Adele Yonkey's never been in my car and I haven't seen her since we were kids. Screw this. I'm leaving."

• • •

The next day Frank called Agent Nichols. "I've been thinking. I'll make a deal with you but only with my attorney present to protect my interests."

Nichols kept his voice matter-of-fact and low while he thought, *let him sweat.* He agreed to meet with Frank at 2 PM the following day. He put down the phone, slapped his hands together and said, "Yes! He's looking to cut a deal!"

• • •

Frank Grady entered the Interrogation Room, rolled his eyes, and took off his coat. FBI Agent Dennis Huff then entered and sniffed the air. If the Interrogation Room was usually kept this hot it would have smelled of sweat but it did not. Agent Huff had observed Frank during his casino play, but this was his first actual contact with Frank Grady.

Attorney Lynn Hamilton was there to represent Frank. She was a criminal attorney, was tall, competent, and just starting out. Her looks and manner impressed, and that was all Frank required of her.

Introductions complete, Agent Nichols turned on the recorder, spoke into it, noted the time of day, the date, the location of the interview, and the names of those present. Then Nichols leaned back in his chair, turned to Frank and asked, "Well now, Mr. Grady, why have you asked for this meeting?"

Frank took a check out of his inside coat pocket, placed it on the table and said, "I've asked my attorney to be present and witness that I'm willing to wager $10,000 against $10,000 from Agent Thomas Nichols of the FBI, that I will provide proof of who killed Adele Yonkey before Agent Nichols is able to accomplish this task."

Dennis Huff picked up the check, looked it over, and said, "It's a Certified Check."

Frank continued, "Let it be noted, that in good faith I have placed a Certified Check for $10,000 on the table. I now challenge Agent Nichols to cover my bet and with the $20,000 going to the winner."

Agent Nichols choked. His mouth was opening and closing—like a goldfish—.

Agent Huff noted flecks of foam in the corners of Nichols's mouth. That reminded him of the fire and brimstone street preacher who had accosted him on his way to this meeting.

Nichols eyebrows reached up into his forehead. Again, he opened his mouth, but no words came out. The spasm passed and getting his voice back, Nichols flinched, choked, and said, "I don't gamble."

It was precisely at that moment that Huff asked himself, *is Nichols epileptic?* Huff said, "Grady, why'd you make this offer?"

"It's a fishing expedition. I wanted to know if Nichols actually thought he had something. He doesn't but empty wagons make more noise than full ones. Nichols is making a lot of noise but that's all he's doing.""

Frank retrieved his check, thanked them for their time, and left.

• • •

Agent Nichols called Frank's home and requested Frank's presence.

The next day Frank arrived, sat, and said, "What's up?"

"Frank, if the lurid details of your family history, along with the

104

details of your sexual relationships with three women, if that ever reaches the press, I suspect this would jar the memories of some. Others might elaborate or even fabricate memories of what they think they've seen. Moral outcry does that sometimes."

Frank stared at Nichols, "More noise. You wish. It's no secret I live with three women. Where'd you get your training Nichols—from a box of crackerjacks?"

Nichols face blossomed red.

"This the best you can come up with? Pathetic." Frank walked out the door thinking, *that man is coming unglued.*

• • •

Agents Adele Wheaten and Dennis Huff were present when Agent Nichols, eyes glittering, declared, "It's frustrating knowing this pervert is out there. He's incredibly arrogant and he's laughing at us. He waited for the day when Annette Tyler turned eighteen before transporting her across Washington State lines and into Idaho."

Huff thought, *Well yeah, he's not stupid.*

Nichols continued, "Two years later, he transported both Annette Tyler and Natalie Fisk across state lines. So . . . we will undertake a war of nerves. If we rattle him, we may provoke him into making a mistake."

On leaving, Huff said, "This is crazy."

Agent Wheaton said, "You don't think we can rattle this guy? . . . neither do I."

Nodding, Huff stated, "I've led men on hazardous missions on three continents. Rattle him? Not going to happen."

CHAPTER SEVENTEEN—Abandoned

Frank was taking his morning run on the bicycle path around Greenlake when FBI Agent Dennis Huff pulled up alongside him. Frank continued running while saying, "Agent Huff, this some kind of planned harassment?"

"Nah. I was ordered to investigate you, to find evidence linking you to Adele Yonkey. I've been watching your Casino play and all I learned is that you usually make a profit. I decided to get closer. You run—so do I."

"Think you'll find anything?"

"I will if there's anything to find. If there's nothing to find then my being close can't hurt you."

"I can't argue with that. What about when you can't keep up?"

"Well now, let's just see if that day ever comes."

The challenge was there. Frank picked up the pace and the shorter legged, heavier built, and older Agent Huff stayed right with him. They circuited the lake three times, almost nine miles, and Huff was still with Frank.

"Enough," Frank said, "You can run alright." He sat himself down on a park bench while Huff flopped down on the other end.

"From time to time I need to get away and run. You need to be seen as investigating me so I'll make a deal with you. If you assume a respectful role as we run then I'll keep you posted as to when and where I'll be running. Can we agree on this?"

"Agreed."

"Okay. I'll be at the foot of Tiger Mountain off Hwy 90 out past Issaquah at 7:30 tomorrow morning."

"I'll be there."

• • •

Frank and Huff charged up the steep incline of Tiger Mountain. On reaching the summit they were gasping for breath. Both were strong runners and while Frank was the stronger on the flat, to his surprise, Dennis was definitely the stronger on the slope. When Frank recovered he said, "I suppose you made a few runs like this in the Marines."

"Uh huh, Try it sometime with a thirty pound pack on your back."

• • •

The shared experience of the tough run up Tiger Mountain promoted a sense of camaraderie. While quenching their thirsts with iced drinks in the town of Issaquah, Frank said, "Tell me about combat."

"I loved it, the adrenaline rush. I never felt more alive or more in harmony with myself and my fellow Marines. The loyalties forged in battle are intense—all the ego bullshit doesn't matter anymore—it's just you and your men. No more bullshit!"

Frank said, "Like living with two or more women."

Huff said, "You putting me on?"

Frank said, "Not like you'd think. There's no room for bullshit there either."

• • •

Seafair Week in Seattle means hydroplane races on Lake Washington, the Seafair Pirates on parade, the Blue Angels flying in formation overhead, and people going crazy. Frank and Dennis Huff were sitting on Frank's dock watching the races. Waves stirred up by the wake of the boats were slapping against the pilings of Frank's dock while the boats were putting out a lot of noise.

"You got a Captain's Mast while going through Boot Camp."

"So you've been looking at my Service Record. Yeah, I walked into that hearing with a contrite look, let one of the Officers get a whiff of my bad breath, and then grimacing, in way of explanation, I said I could taste the poison from my tonsils.

"On enlisting I'd signed a waiver allowing the Navy to fix the problem but they still hadn't done it. So, instead of going to the Brig for punching out Dandy, I was transferred to the base hospital where they took out what was left of my tonsils, which, by that time, had rotted down to the roots. I was told that the surgery, for a tonsillectomy, had been difficult—they kept me in the hospital for five days. Then I was transferred to a new Boot Company."

"So, you worked your tonsils to get out of Brig time."

"I did. Killed two birds with one stone. My breath was sweeter and I did better at getting along in my second Company."

"You got through it."

"They didn't know what to do with me. I didn't fit in, but I was strong, my test scores were high, I was a decent and self-taught accountant, and in time the chip came off my shoulder."

• • •

In September the rains came and enveloped Seattle in a constant wet drizzle. Frank received a call from Artie Karp's son Michael who said that Artie had cancer, did not have much time left, and would like to see Frank.

Frank caught the next flight to New York. On arrival, he took a cab directly to the hospital. Artie's men were on the hall and the door to his room. Artie was shrunken and looked like a skeleton, but he was alert and pleased to see Frank.

Frank admitted, "I don't have that many friends and I sure don't like losing this one."

Artie replied, "Yeah, me too. Mostly it was the business. I neglected my friends and mostly my wife and children. Don't make that mistake Frankie. Spend as much time with your family as you can. I've made amends with my wife and children, we've made our peace with each other, but I should have done things differently." Again, Artie thanked Frank for coming, then said, "I'm tired. I have to sleep now." As Frank headed for the door, he heard Artie say, "You take care of yourself Frankie."

Artie died in his sleep that night.

• • •

On that cold, blustery day and after the funeral, Frank talked with Artie's son Michael, who was not in the life and was a prominent Park Avenue ophthalmologist. Michael spoke of Artie's early history, growing up on New York's Delancey Street. Artie's early years were much like Frank's early years.

The first time Artie and Frank saw each other, they knew they were friends. Now Frank understood the why of it. Over the years, Artie and Frank had not seen much of each other, but they always thought of each other as simpatico, as friends.

Frank attended Artie's funeral, as did his family and prominent mob figures, while the ever-present FBI watched and filmed all who were there.

• • •

Overnight, the streets on Mercer Island had received a faint covering of snow. Frank was in flight from New York to Las Vegas when FBI Agent Edward Addison walked through the slush to Frank's door. A morose-looking and polite man, he asked if he could speak with the women of the house. He looked weighted down and like the bearer of bad news. Melina let him in. Addison took a packet of photos out of his briefcase, sighed and said, "Have you heard the name Nola James or seen this woman? Take your time to look and think about it." They had not. He sighed, took out another photo saying, "Alli Trevelyn, have you ever seen or heard of her?"

All told, Agent Addison showed the women photos of five women, and asked when and if they had seen any of them. They had not. Annette asked, "Who are they?"

Agent Addison sighed wistfully and said, "They are women who disappeared after meeting Frank. We had hoped that you might know something. Thank you for your time."

They watched as Agent Addison, shoulders sagging as he slumped down to his car.

In his car, crossing the Lake Washington Bridge, as he was driving away, Agent Addison sat up tall, pumped his fist in the air, and shouted, "Yes!"

. . .

Seattle Times posted what they classified as an FBI Official Report. It stated:

The killer of Adele Yonkey is very probably a serial killer and one who has grown more disciplined over time. The killer is someone highly intelligent, highly mobile, and able to be in many locations without raising questions, he is probably married, has children, and is able to flaunt an unconventional but successful lifestyle. The method of display of the victim's body indicates that the offender is someone experienced with the use of bondage ties, is probably physically strong and athletic, and the product of a dysfunctional family. He has very likely experienced abandonment by a distant or uncaring mother and a physically abusive and/ or absent father.

. . .

Those in Seattle's news media were quick to associate that profile with what they knew of Frank Grady and they descended on the women and children like a school of piranha—each scrambling for the first bite.

. . .

Then the women received a visit from Child Protective Services. After they left, Annette said, "I don't believe any of this but I do believe that if this goes any further, we could lose the children. The kids come first and we need to protect them."

Melina nodded, picked up the phone and called her father. When he picked up, Melina reported all.

"I don't know what's going on, Wassef said, "but you and the children are in danger so I will be getting you and them out of harm's way while I find out what is going on!"

. . .

That very day, from North Africa, Mister Wassef Hamdi orchestrated the evacuation of the women and children. They were flown by private jet to Hamburg where Wassef met their flight and finalized the last steps to having the women and children transported to a safe haven in Villars, Switzerland. Then Wassef flew back to Africa. All this he accomplished in less than 48 hours.

• • •

Frank arrived home with Artie Karp's advice still ringing in his ears. Artie had said,

"Spend as much time with your family as you can."

The stillness in the house was eerie. The women and children were not there.

There was a note that read:

Frank,

To protect the children, we are taking them away.

• • •

Reading this, Frank's legs trembled. He ran for the bathroom and dropped his drawers, his bowels rumbled to life and then, feeling himself ready to pass out, he laid down on the bathroom floor.

It was dark when he arose. He looked at his watch, and saw that it was 11 PM. He went to the refrigerator and took out the plate of baklava packaged in Saran Wrap.

Sitting at the kitchen table, nibbling on a piece of baklava, Frank said to himself, *and the condemned man ate a hearty meal.*

• • •

Frank received a letter from Melina asking that, to protect the children, he should sign the enclosed document agreeing to an Annulment of Marriage. He signed it. Frank thought, *The final straw. If it had been Agent Nichols's intention to destroy my family, he has succeeded admirably.*

CHAPTER EIGHTEEN—The Edifice

Frank was sitting on his deck when Wassef showed up and said, "You have any coffee?"

"There's a fresh pot on the stove. You know the way."

Wassef returned with coffee and stood behind Frank for a time. "You don't seem alarmed at having me standing behind you."

"No."

"You're a trusting soul."

"If you wanted me dead I'd be dead and you wouldn't be here. So why are you here?"

Wassef didn't answer.

"The women and I built an edifice, a social structure based on protocols that were stronger than the sum total of us all. When that fake profile came down, if the women had followed the protocols, said they were afraid for the children, I would have told them to take the children and run. I would not have gone with them—but even so, emotionally, the family would have remained intact."

Wassef nodded. "It wasn't the women, it was pressure from the outside that broke up your family."

"With all the attacks on me personally, and all the attacks on the family, we weathered the storm until the day the women abandoned the protocols. That was the day my world fell apart! Leaving like that—without a hello, a goodbye, or even a kiss my ass—the whole damn thing is unforgivable."

"You sound bitter."

"Guilty as charged!"

. . .

Agent Kimberly Wheaten reported to the office of Agent Nichols who said, "With Frank's children and their mothers now out of the country, Frank's attentions will wander. Frank Grady is a seductive sleezeball who's never seen you; it's time to turn the tables and seduce the seducer. As distasteful as it may be—you will get up close with this man."

. . .

Frank was in the grips of an agitated depression. For two weeks he seldom left the house, spent a reclusive and excessive amount of time pounding on the heavy bag and staring at pictures of the women and children.

The day came finally, when he said to himself, *time to get moving*. He set his alarm for eight AM, awoke to an empty house, fixed breakfast, and made his way to Greenlake. Three mornings later Frank finished his run with a sprint that left him bent over, hands on thighs, and gasping for breath. He was breathing a little easier when an attractive and breathless woman pulled up alongside him. Gasping, she said, "When you ran by I challenged myself to keep pace with you. I couldn't have run ten more steps." She had light brown hair, brown eyes, and a slender and killer body. Swallowing, she extended her hand and said, "My name's Kimberly Wheaten."

He took her sturdy small hand saying, "Frank Grady."

"Buy me an espresso and I won't bore you with my life's story."

He grinned, "How about we run together tomorrow, say 9 AM? Then I'll buy you an espresso." Frank was wondering, *is she a news-hound or a cop?*

Kimberly Wheaten said, "Deal."

. . .

Retired Detective Phil Baade was troubled. He had pulled the boy Frank Grady off the Tacoma Narrows Bridge railing, and it troubled him to think that the boy he saved could be the one who killed Adele Yonkey. He had heard through the police grapevine that an anonymous phone call had pointed a finger at Frank Grady, and watching for developments,

Detective Baade concluded the FBI's current investigation, like their initial investigation, was going nowhere.

He decided to deal himself in. He took a risk—approached Frank at his home and said, "You remember me?

"You took me off that railing."

"Did I make a mistake?"

"You didn't. I'm going to forget you asked that question."

Detective Baade nodded, "The boy I took off that railing wouldn't have killed Adele Yonkey and posed her like that. We're probably the only two people who believe that. I want to show you something."

Placing copies of the Adele Yonkey crime scene photos in front of Frank, he watched for Frank's reaction.

"Oh Jesus! You're not supposed to have these are you?"

"No I'm not. I was the initial responding officer but because the body was found on Indian Land the Feds took over the case."

Frank looked at the photos, carefully handed them back, and shook his head. "Hell of a way to end up. Whoever did this would have had no respect for Adele. She was a modest, dignified creature. Bad enough he killed her—posing her like that was disrespectful—but for her having been posed like that the case would have been long forgotten.

Phil Baade nodded.

Suddenly startled, Frank said, "Hey! Hold on *just a damn minute!* Let me see those photos. The ring. It's missing—I remember, she always had a ring on her right second finger!"

"So you saying whoever did this took a souvenir?"

"Check with her family. It was a slender and long black onyx ring that ran along the finger. Detective Baade, the FBI's still looking at me and so they're getting nowhere. If you're willing to work this case I'm willing to pay."

"I'm willing to work the case but I'm unwilling to accept payment. However, you can cover my expenses."

"Deal!"

• • •

Frank and Kimberly ran the 2.9 miles around Greenlake. For almost the first full lap, Kimberly kept up the pace. Then she faded while Frank finished his run with an all-out sprint.

The two of them had espressos together, while Phil Baade, with his sister Judy, watched and waited. They tailed Kimberly to the parking garage at the Federal Building. Judy jumped out of Phil's car and entered the Federal Building's main entrance. She tracked Kimberly's movements to the office of FBI Agent Tom Nichols.

• • •

It was five days later when Frank informed Kimberly, "I usually make the Tiger Mountain run with Dennis Huff but he's away on business. Tomorrow morning I'll make the run up Tiger Mountain. It's a tough run." Looking down at her slender legs he reported, "Running up that path is hard on the thighs. I enjoy running with you and having espressos afterwards but this is one run you will want to skip."

Kimberly volunteered, "Wrong. I'd like to give it a try."

• • •

At 8 AM Kimberly was standing on the southwest corner of Third and Union. Frank pulled up to the curb, and flipped open the passenger-side door. Kimberly folded her umbrella and took the passenger seat. She thought, *Thank God there are agents in the car following.*

Exiting Seattle on Interstate 90, and after already passing the exit for Highway 405, an alarmed Kimberly, keeping her tone casual, asked, "Why are we pulling off Interstate 90?"

"Breakfast." Frank was relaxed and took his time with a large breakfast while Kimberly fidgeted. This was not how things had been planned and other agents were already set in place in the wet brush along the trail up Tiger Mountain.

Frank and Kimberly were parked at the base of Tiger Mountain when the light rains turned into a deluge. Frank said, "Let's sit here awhile—see if the rain lightens up."

An hour later, the rain did let up, and they began their run up the trail on the east side of Tiger Mountain. After the first twenty yards, Kimberly gasped, "This is tougher than I thought." Ten yards further, she spotted a small red rag tied to a bush. The red rag signaled to Kimberly, *go no further.* She slowed to a walk and said, "You were right. I can't go on."

Frank didn't believe her and had to restrain the impulse to eye the brush on the east side of the path. He suspected, rightly, that FBI Agents were lurking there. What he said was, "It's a tough run. I'll meet you on the way down."

Frank is not a casual runner. The more challenging the run the more he strives to meet the challenge. Plus, in this instance, knowing he was being set up, he was pumping adrenaline, and in the drizzle of that wet day Frank was comforted with the thought of how many FBI Agents would be sitting in wet brush in that first fifty yards, them having already sat through an hours deluge and now all waiting for him to make a move so they could rush out like Honest Woodsmen, rescue Little Red Riding Hood, and put stones in the Wolf's belly.

Frank finished the tough run to the top of Tiger Mountain. Then, curious to see what would happen next, he began a risky down-hill trot.

Kimberly said, "Seeing you loping down that steep slope made me afraid you'd take a header and injure yourself."

"Your concern is comforting."

Kimberly eyed him. She wasn't sure . . . was he being sarcastic?

• • •

Frank was driving Kimberly back to where he'd picked her up. He was aware they were being escorted with one car taking the position behind Frank, then dropping back while the other tail moved up. Frank thought, *Sorry to disappoint you boys.*

• • •

Kimberly said, "Frank, we've been seeing each other for three weeks and you've never made a pass at me. I'm not complaining—if you're not interested then you're not interested, but I have to wonder what's going on."

Rubbing the back of his neck, Frank said, "It's too soon. When you showed up I suspected you were either FBI or an investigative reporter and so I had you followed. You're FBI. It was a wise man who said: Keep your friends close and your enemies even closer. So you being FBI wouldn't have slowed me down. It's something else. There's no lack of interest or attraction but I can't do this. I'm too raw—I was the richest of men and then, all at once, I lost the mothers and our beautiful children."

"It's too soon? It's that simple?"

Tilting his head and grimacing, he said, "It's that simple. I have nothing but contempt for Agent Nichols. What kind of a sick- son-of-a-bitch does it take to assign a woman to cozy up to someone he believes is a serial killer? If I was what Nichols thinks I am you'd be dead—Kimberly, you're in a tough spot. If you admit your cover's been blown you'll end up being transferred to a going nowhere position in East Nowhere."

"You think?"

"I think. I'm willing to play along as if I didn't know, but Agent Nichols is sinking; he'll be looking for someone to share the blame and that puts you in a lose-lose situation."

• • •

Kimberly took the risk, reported to Agent Nichols, "My cover's been blown and I have neither seen nor heard anything that would indicate that Frank Grady committed that crime. I don't think he's the one."

"Your gullibility," Nichols said, "your lack of critical judgment, has allowed this scumbag to seduce you."

• • •

Nichols then wrote a scathing fitness report and Kimberly was reassigned to a minor clerical and going nowhere position within the lower bowel of the FBI bureaucracy. In plain English—she was demoted from her position as a Supervising Agent to doing what she considered as the shit-work, necessary shit-work but still . . . while her father urged her to stick it out. Kimberly said, "No way!" and handed in her resignation.

Frank was not surprised at her demotion—despite all his own losses, surprised he still cared.

CHAPTER NINETEEN—Frank Retaliates

Retired Detective Phil Baade was there to meet Frank when he finished his run. Phil said, "Adele Yonkey's car was abandoned in the parking lot at the Northgate Mall. I suspect whoever killed her would not have taken the ferry and run the risk of being seen and remembered. Her body was dropped off on Croft Road. Round-trip that's more than 150 miles and the killer would have stopped for gas. The FBI checked gas cards for that morning but I suspect they were looking only for your name." He said to himself, *I followed Frank's career from boyhood, and when I went over that same gas material a name jumped out at me. If I give Frank the name he might go looking and screw up my investigation.*

What Detective Baade said was, "I'm looking at someone and that's all you need to know. If the FBI already investigated and cleared this guy then you're still the best suspect we have."

"You're not going to tell me what you've found are you?"

"I am not."

"Thanks a lot."

· · ·

Frank had driven north on University Avenue. He was stopped three cars back from the stoplight, had left an open space between his car and the car ahead of him, and when the light turned green

Frank made a sudden U turn directly in front of the oncoming traffic. Going the other way he recognized FBI Agent White beating his fist on the steering wheel. Frank had already found the tracking device attached to his car.

He rolled the window down and plopped the tracking device into the bed of a pickup in line to enter Interstate Five North.

Agent White reported having been made and ditched by Frank Grady. Agent Nichols mobilized everyone on the assumption that Frank was making a run for it and heading for Canada. Nichols thought— *mission accomplished; his first mistake. Even if he makes it I'm shed of this damned case!*

The FBI was chasing up Interstate Five with orders not to apprehend Frank until he attempts to cross into Canada. His pursuers were zeroed in on the tracking device previously attached to his car. Other agents were in place to apprehend Frank when he tried to cross into Canada.

When the tracking device indicated an exit off Interstate Five and into Marysville, the FBI followed. It was embarrassing to discover that they had been tracking a tacky Chevy pickup now parked in a Safeway parking lot. They confiscated the tracking device and reported in.

• • •

The Seattle Channel Five Evening News released a report stating, "Yesterday, Mr. Frank Grady, a person of interest to the FBI, withdrew a large sum of money from his account and has now disappeared."

The newsroom then showed surveillance photo's of Frank and the newscaster said, "The FBI is asking for the public's help in locating this man."

• • •

Frank had entered Caesars Palace only minutes before that Newscast. He took a seat in a high stakes poker game. Between hands, the Pit Boss said, "Frank, the FBI's been on TV asking for the public's help in locating you."

Frank did not appear alarmed. Nodding, he said, "For sure, they need fresh leadership."

Frank had held the FBI and Agents such as Dennis Huff in high regard but this war was personal, and had been initiated by former school classmate and now FBI Director Alvin Frugate.

"The present FBI leadership," Frank said, "needs all the help they can get since they would have to use both hands in order to locate their own ass."

Someone laughed and said, "Deal the cards."

• • •

Frank's attention did not waver, never in his life had he been more focused, and except for bathroom breaks, he played poker for 20 hours straight, wired his winnings to his Seattle account, slept for eight hours, and caught a flight back to Seattle.

• • •

Agent Nichols had embarrassed the FBI. He entered into a series of Petite Mal seizures, and had to be hospitalized. He was finished, the second FBI Agent to bite the dust in this case.

• • •

FBI Director Frugate pointed out that Agent Nichols had not been disabled when assigned to the Adele Yonkey case. However, the base of Frugate's support was crumbling.

Huff, sitting out on Frank's dock, said, "Frank, how'd you know when that Newscast would be aired? No answer? This screw-up has Frugate skating on thin ice."

Frank shrugged.

"All that domesticity —I know you miss the family now—but back then I could picture you feeling a need, from time to time, to get away from all that domestic responsibility."

Frank continued to stare out over the lake and without turning he said, "Mostly I loved it, the domestic bliss, but there were times when I felt the weight of it. When I needed to refocus, I would go for solitary runs to recharge my batteries. Adjusting to all the changes, all the closeness, put me on a learning curve and by the time we had my first child I couldn't imagine life without my family. Hell of a jolt losing my family. Losing Grandma and Grandpa was bad, we've never talked about that but you read the files. The culmination of all the bad days was learning the women and the children had jumped ship."

• • •

Former FBI Agent Kimberly Wheaten called from Missoula, Montana. She wanted to know if it would be OK to visit Frank. He said, "Tomorrow afternoon would be fine. I'll fix dinner."

Kimberly arrived at 3 PM. She looked frayed around the edges. She said, "I drove in from Arlington rather than fly because I needed time to think. I haven't been sleeping well. Some of my former colleagues still believe you murdered Adele Yonkey and orchestrated the death of Agent Nichols. That and other questions have been troubling me."

Frank said, "I didn't murder Adele and I didn't orchestrate Nichols's death—Period. I like you Kimberly, but you bring this up again and I won't much like you. You look wrung out so I suggest you take a soak in the tub and a nap in the hammock out on the deck. It's shaded and this time of day a cool breeze comes in off the lake. I'll come and get you when dinner's ready."

• • •

Frank called her at 6:15. They had an evening meal of small steaks along with asparagus, Spanish rice, and a small dinner salad. After dinner they retired to the deck and Frank said, "What brings you here?"

Kimberly dropped her eyes. "You asked so I'll tell you. Agent Nichols assigned me to get close to you and establish a relationship. He believed you were a dangerous serial killer. I should have been scared out of my wits, but instead I looked forward to gaining his approval. I was grateful for the assignment and eager to get started. You once said something that still haunts me. You said I had a zealous loyalty and you voiced recognition of my having surrendered up my life to the FBI. How could you know that?"

Looking out over the water, he said, "Jesus Kimmy, think on it; how could I not know? I recognized in you a need to surrender to some-thing or some-one."

"Uh huh. I had a duty to report that you knew I was FBI. You tempted me to abort my duty and not report it. God was I tempted."

"You did report it and Nichols canned you."

"I don't need reminding."

· · ·

Evening shadows were beginning to march across the outside deck. Frank stated, "No question. You were a good little FBI soldier. The Military talks of instilling in its young men and women character, honor and courage. Yet they give no recognition to these qualities as a surrender to the ethic of the Corps. They define such acts as self-actualizing rather than as self- sacrificing and they're right—surrender to something greater than ourselves, whether it's the FBI, the Marines, a God, is self-actualizing, potentially one of our nobler attributes—but you surrendered yourself up to the Bureau that was intent on convicting me of a crime you intuitively knew I never committed—when you have lingering doubts then your surrender needs to becomes even more frenzied, like the German people's fervid adoration of Adolf Hitler to quiet their own doubts about the man."

Kimberly swallowed. "You hit hard Frank . . . but I deserve it. You never surrendered to anything. You always did things your own way."

"Don't believe it! Like everyone else, I'd like to delude myself that I'm a rugged individualist. The truth is I surrendered myself up to my Grandfather's ideology, the way he taught me. We don't like to admit it but we're all sheep looking for our shepherd to point us on our way. Only the psychopath escapes into total autonomy, and that is what makes him a psychopath."

Kimberly looked lost in thought . . . she asked, "Would it be okay for me to stay the night?"

"Take the second bedroom at the top of the stairs."

· · ·

Kimberly came down the stairs in a shapeless flannel gown that stretched to the floor.

Frank put down his book.

Kimberly looked out the window. She turned to him and said, "When I was assigned to your case, Amy Phillips took me to a Greek Restaurant in Pioneer Square. We lingered over coffee at an outdoor table and waited for your arrival with the women from your house. You took an outside table at the restaurant directly across the square from us."

Amy identified Melina as your wife and Annette and Natalie as your common-law wives. We had a directional listening device and eavesdropped from across the square. I had assumed you were some kind of a sociopathic Svengali who enslaved women against their will and as someone who would need to be stopped before you enslaved other women. I thought that any woman who'd invite this must be a weakling or a wacko. Yet when I listened to taped interviews of Annette and Natalie, I realized they were not at all what I'd imagined. I admired their character. They thrived as part of a ménage. So I ask you, what is there about surrender that would attract women such as this?"

"Surrender to the values of the group is an absolute necessity if the group is to survive and that surrender is what allowed our species to conquer the world. My family fell apart when they abandoned our protocols. Artie Karp, a gentleman I knew well, told the tale of his grandfather, an elderly Jew who insisted that there was no need to flee, that the German people were a civilized people.

"He was right. The Germans were a civilized people and therefore they surrendered to the group concept of a 'Jewish Problem.' Artie's grandfather, being a 'civilized' man, did not resist as he was herded into the gas chamber."

"What you're saying troubles me . . .. Frank, are you trying to seduce me?"

"Maybe . . . and then maybe not." Kimberly retreated to her room.

• • •

Kimberly returned. She was in her robe. "Frank, I'm ready. I'm yours if you want me."

Frank's hand engulfed her small hand—she did not resist as he led her up the stairs and into the bedroom.

. . .

Frank was preparing breakfast when Kimberly came into the kitchen dressed only in one of his shirts and with the sleeves rolled up.

"So," Frank said, "this is what you want?"

"I can't believe I'm saying this. Yes. This is what I want."

. . .

Melina called from Zurich and informed Frank she was studying at the Jungian Institute.

"Uh huh. How are the kids?"

"The children are doing well in school and they're picking up French quicker than their mothers. We can't keep up with them. They're unhappy some of the time, get misty-eyed and don't know who to blame."

Choking, Frank said, "Kimberly, take the phone."

. . .

When Frank came out of the bathroom, Kimberly said, "Melina asked me if I was going to marry you?"

"And you said?"

"How can I? He hasn't stopped bleeding."

CHAPTER TWENTY—The Secret Service Approaches

Sandy Peck's mother said, "Sandy, you study those girls. You look until you find the one who comes across as the most wholesome, totally honest and trustworthy, and you study her. Study her speech, her mannerisms, the way she moves, the unaffected way she carries herself, her attitudes, what she believes, learn those things, copy them, and that, along with your looks and that terrific body, will make you a great con artist.

Sandy found her. She was wholesome more than pretty, admired by everyone, and Sandy duplicated her every move, every unaffected gesture.

• • •

Frank was dressed for a run when he looked out the window and recognized Dennis Huff approaching. Why were they sending him back?

Answering the door, Frank said, "Mister Dennis Huff. It's been awhile. Is the FBI taking another shot at hooking me up with the Adele Yonkey murder? No?"

"No."

"Well then, let me not be inhospitable. Come on in."

Dennis came in, and looking around, he noted the place looked the same but it didn't feel the same.

Frank cracked a smile. "By the way, You FBI are supposed to look interchangeable—tall, athletic, wearing business suits and shades. Now you stand before me, short, stocky, wearing a blue blazer, gray slacks, loafers, a clip-on bow tie, those rimless glasses, your shrapnel scarred face . . . you're out of uniform. You look more like a Marine on Shore Leave."

"Thank you. Always nice to be recognized. I could have worn my FBI uniform but I switched to my Marine On-Shore-Leave uniform. How you like the pink bowtie? Nice touch eh?"

"Damn slick move Dennis. In that getup no one would suspect you of being FBI."

"I'm proud to say that I still look, think, and feel like a US Marine."

"Uh huh. Once a Marine always a Marine?"

"That's it! At first glance you look more FBI than I do. But those eyes—since the women and kids left—they give you away. You can't hide the fact you came up from the mean streets . . . not anymore."

"Dennis, how much do you know about J. Edgar's self-induced blind spot regarding organized crime? Did you know he ignored organized crime for years so he could concentrate on going after headlines, after communists, and Public Enemies like John Dillinger, Pretty Boy Floyd, and Baby Face Nelson? Hoover's gone but the beat goes on—and there I was—headline potential there and the FBI came after me."

Dennis looked out over the yard, out over the lake.

"Huff, you know . . . As a Marine you had my respect. But you crossed me up when you signed on with the FBI. I can't imagine what kind of a personal crisis would have prompted you, a Decorated Marine, to sink so low as to become an FBI Agent."

Huff put on his puzzled look. "Well now, how am I supposed to take that? Is this supposed to be a complement or an insult? For your information I re-upped with the FBI so I could spend time with my daughter. I did my duty as a US Marine and mostly out of the country. Incidentally, how come Director Frugate has such a hard-on for you?"

"I never talked about that . . . a long time ago, school days, I wandered early into the first afternoon class. Miss Weeks was spraying the leaves of her potted plant and wiping them down. Then she took an eyedropper and fed the plant.

"Seeing this, I thought, *Jesus. That's what they do with Alvin Frugate.* He sits around like a damn potted plant, expecting others to water and feed him. And the weird thing is, they do—all of them—all this while I was catching shit from everyone.

"I said, "Alvin, I bet that when you were a baby people competed for the privilege of changing your diaper. Weird thing is, they still do. How you do this?"

"Frank," Alvin said, "I'm never going to be tall, slender, or handsome. I'm nearsighted and need glasses, but as an infant I was the only male in a household with a mother and two older sisters who doted on me. In that setting I could expect to be taken care of and I was. Expecting to be taken care of became an expectation, a habit with me, the same way catching shit became a habit with you."

"I caught my breath and said, 'My hat's off to you Alvin. I bet you worked on that little speech for a month—sounds great—reasonable and honest. Alvin, I saw Burl Ives in a movie and his character kept using the word *mendacity*. I looked it up. You're good Alvin. No one, not Miss Weeks, not our classmates, no one except me recognizes the mendacity you hide so well.'"

"You said that?"

"I did. And Alvin's apple-dumpling expression was superseded by an expression of pure malice."

Dennis shook his head, "Hard to believe."

"Believe. That bastard Frugate used the office of the FBI to hurt me, and with no regard for the collateral damage it would do to the women and children."

• • •

Sitting on a park bench after having finished their run, Frank said, "OK Dennis, enough dancing. Why are you here?"

"You have some talents the Service can't duplicate. I stayed in touch with Kimberly after she resigned. She said something about having to check things out with you. When I asked what, she didn't answer. The next thing I knew she was living with you; how did you manage to recruit her? "

"You just changed the subject."

"So I did. How did you recruit her?"

"Dennis, for Christ's sake, that's an illusion! From the first to the last, I never recruited any of them—they recruited me."

"You bullshitting me Frank?"

"For real Dennis, why have they sent you back?"

"My superiors are considering making you an offer."

"Oh Jesus! In exchange for what?"

"In exchange for nothing."

"Something for nothing—like the Trojan horse—I do remember that old caution: Beware of Greeks bearing gifts."

• • •

Huff reported back to Secret Service Supervisor Kickman. "Frank seemed hostile when I showed up. Yet, during that interview, everything seemed to shift. For sure I was supposed to get him talking."

"And did you?"

"We danced around each other. Underneath his histrionics, Frank was giving me nothing new. There was nothing we could use, and it was him giving me a hard time and scoping me out."

Agent Kickman nodded. "Years ago, when I was still a stunning young blond, I was assigned to come on to Frank. I was not into jogging. He was on his morning run out on Mercer Island when I drove up alongside him and asked for directions. He looked me over and then gave me the directions. I said, I'll never remember all that."

He shrugged.

"I said, if you show me then I will drive you anywhere you want to go, and he said, 'I don't ride with the police.'"

"I didn't see any use in denying it, so I asked how he knew and he said, 'Your clothing is casual and good quality but not top quality. Meanwhile, the car you're driving's a classic, top of the line, and the key in the ignition is a single key. The car's a loaner from a dealership and you needed other keys on the key ring.'"

Agent Joanna Kickman continued, "Huff, your former FBI Supervisor Kimberly Wheaten is now living with Frank Grady. How did he recruit her?"

Dennis Huff shrugged. "Street smarts. He studies people and

doesn't miss much."

"That's no answer. I need to know more about this man before I make him an offer. See if you can determine how he Svengalied those women into surrendering to him."

CHAPTER TWENTY-ONE—Sandy earns her Doctorate

In New York's Broadway district, the lecher saw the girl through the café window. Her brow was furrowed as she recounted her money, three fives and two ones. She paused to take a bite of the hamburger in front of her, then for the umpteenth time, she recounted her money as if hoping to come up with a different amount.

The lecher said to himself, *she's about sixteen, a good-looker and has terrific boobs plus she may not be too bright. My lucky day.* Entering the café he sat across from her and was wearing his kindly face. He had a practiced patience and waited for her to look up.

When she raised her eyes she saw a medium-sized man, 45 years old, with a friendly and concerned look. "I couldn't help but notice," he said, "that you have troubles. I don't usually do things like this, but . . . is there some way I can help?"

One tear dropped out of her right eye and ran down her cheek. "Those are the first kind words I've heard in five days."

The lecher had a moment of actually feeling virtuous. The girl confessed that she owed four days back rent and had been locked out of her room and they were holding her suitcase and clothes until she paid her bill.

• • •

The lecher gave her five twenties and waited outside the hotel while she talked to the desk clerk. He saw her then head for the stairs. Five minutes later he entered the hotel and headed for room 218 on the second floor. Then he discovered there *was* no room 218 on the second floor.

The con known as the Murphy Game is usually worked by a male/female team. Sandy had successfully worked her one woman version of the game three times that day but it was risky with her alone and without having male muscle for protection. It was time to be moving on. She bought a bus ticket to San Diego. Surprisingly, while she had lived outside the law all her young life and was no innocent, she was still a virgin.

Sandy Peck had a generous smile and eyes that flashed a sparkling innocence. With the coming of puberty her figure, coupled with her youth, and her appearance of innocence, had served as the distraction that allowed her mother and her mother's partner, the High-Assed Kid, to pull off their scams. The Kid was now dead and Sandy's mother was in lockup.

• • •

Sandy took up the run from Mexico City to San Diego with plastic containers of cocaine up her rectum and vagina—she had sacrificed her hymen to a plastic container—and having been seen one too many times on the run from San Diego to Seattle, she was being detained in juvenile lockup.

Dennis Huff arranged for Sandy's transfer from the Juvenile Hall to the miss-named Echo Glen Children's Shelter; it was a detention facility, not a shelter. Dennis showed up at Frank's still shaking his head in wonderment at what he saw as a dysfunctional Juvenile Justice system.

Staring out over the lake Huff said, "Counselor Davis, smug little shit that he is, said to me that the young men and women are locked in separate rooms at night, but the cottages, being coed during the day, allow our young men and women to learn how to relate to others of the opposite sex."

Dennis, as a former Marine Officer, knew young men. "You're not doing any girl a favor by having them learn how to relate to the creepy little sleazeballs I met today. The girls are even worse. They smile nice and put on the helpless act and so they get away with even more shit than the boys so by the time they actually do get locked up they've already got away with so much shit they're a real mess!"

"You amaze me Dennis. You actually expected the Juvenile Justice System to make sense? I thought you were smarter than that!"

Huff shook his head. "I said that if those kids came out of here with no experience at all in relating to the opposite sex they'd be ahead of the game rather than if they came out handicapped with the learned knowledge of how to relate to those charming little sleazeballs, male and female, that I met today. You let a creepy girl connect with a creepy boy and something even creepier is going to happen!"

Frank nodded. "The system's screwed. No question." Looking out over the lake Frank continued, "You're good for me Huff. You force me to look back and recover those things, good and bad, that I've blanked out."

Huff's eyebrows lifted. "I've been sent here to use you and now you're using me?"

Waving his hand dismissively, Frank said, "Huff, it's the nature of the beast. After all, what else are friends for?"

• • •

Kimberly Wheaten, Huff's former FBI Supervisor, formerly authoritative and business-like, but now compliant, wearing makeup and alluringly dressed, greeted Dennis Huff at the door and served him coffee.

Huff's last visit had been twelve days ago. Now he said, "Kimberly, when you were my Senior Officer, you looked good, but you never looked this good."

"I know. I never thought I'd say this, but I like this better. Agent Nichols never suspected he was letting the Genie out of the bottle when he ordered me to get makeup, sexy clothes, and come-on to Frank."

Dennis thought, *that backfired . . . big time. The FBI giveth as the FBI taketh away.*

"Frank's on the phone," she said. "Wait. He'll show up."

"Kimberly, I don't understand how this happened? Why?"

Eyes flashing, she said, "How? Why? You were present on the day Nichols assigned me to come on to Frank and establish a relationship with him. I did, and I found no evidence linking Frank to Adele Yonkey. There was not one single link. I found nothing that would indicate Frank had any connection with that crime. When I communicated my conviction that it had not been Frank who committed the crime, Nichols went insane—and assigned my career to the toilet."

• • •

Frank entered with a cup of coffee and sat.

Kimberly took a seat on a floor cushion at Frank's feet. It pleased her to lean against his legs as he stroked her hair.

Huff said, "I don't get it . . . you treat her like a pet poodle!"

"I've lost my family and I can't do the family bit again. One day Kimberly will want to have children. When that day comes you could be the one, but for now she belongs to me."

Then Huff saw Kimberly and Frank exchange a look electric. Without foreshadowing, it became obvious that the two of them were aroused.

Softly, Frank said, "Huff, go home. We can talk later."

Huff dropped his eyes, shook his head, and headed for the door.

• • •

On his next visit, after they finished tossing around the football, Huff said, "I spoke with your old school Principal Mr. Pearson."

"Huh! He's still alive. How's he doing?"

"He's quite elderly and in a wheelchair . . . but he remembers you Frank."

"Damn he ought to! He's the one expelled me! Eventually, I joined the Navy."

Huff nodded, "Should have been the Marines. With your stamina and guts you'd have made a hell of a Marine."

• • •

Huff had not slept well. Being around Frank tended to shake up some of his previously held beliefs—not many, but some. "Frank, I never bought the Nichols Evaluation of Kimberly. That was a shitty thing he did. But still, you hooked Kimberly into coming in with you. How did you do that?"

"Dennis, are you willing to talk to me about how J. Edger Hoover, the first FBI Director, and Frank Costello, the so-called Prime Minister of the Mob, how they became friends and were meeting in New York and Washington?"

"Is this true?"

"People have reported seeing the two of them together at the race track, on a bench in Central Park, and in the lobby of the Waldorf-Astoria. Some might have tried to make something out of Hoover placing bets at the ten dollar window while sending an FBI Agent to place bets for him at the hundred dollar window . . . but, there's probably nothing to it."

Frank poured each of them another cup of coffee.

"Yeah, Dennis said, "Probably nothing to it . . .." Huff sat down his coffee. "Meeting with Frank Costello in Central Park and the Waldorf-Astoria, probably doing research . . .."

"Yeah, and in the name of justice, who are we to make judgments?"

"What's justice Frank? That's not clear."

"You're not clear on what justice is? You surprise me Dennis. Justice is when the rich man is proven innocent of the crime while the poor man is hung by the neck until dead."

"I'm glad you cleared that up for me. If I had a wife, I'd rush home right now and share that with her."

• • •

Frank quizzed Huff about his Judo training.

"Frank, if the two of us were to fight, do you really think you could take me?"

"Dennis, you're a short, stocky grappler. I'm a fighter, have a terrific punch, and if I hit you first I'll bury you! I'm pretty nasty, but even so, if you got your hands on me first, chances are you'd bury me! It would probably depend on which of us were feeling the meanest that day.

"For a magical time I was a family man and a reputable businessman. It didn't last. My former classmate Alvin Frugate, as FBI Director, inserted the key and gave it a quarter turn to the left. That opened the door and I lost my family. It's all irreconcilable.

Huff nodded. "Uh huh. It sickens me when I think about your children's hurt and confusion. And the women . . . well . . . I'm not defending them, but I do understand. After they left, you weren't making much noise, but for a time you looked like you were ready to explode."

"Yeah. It could have happened at a-n-y minute!"

"You blame Director Frugate for this?"

"I do. And I'm going to bring that rat bastard Frugate down someday!"

CHAPTER TWENTY-TWO—The Recruitment

Huff said, "Frank, let me give you a hypothetical situation. Suppose a man kidnaps a young girl, strips her, chains her to the wall, uses her every way he can think of, tortures her periodically, and says he's growing tired of her . . . what's going to happen next?"

Frank turned his head slowly and stared at Huff . . .. Quietly he said, "Hypothetical my ass!"

"You're right. Not hypothetical. The girl's now living with Agent Joanna Kickman. Her abductor's on the loose and it's hoped that once we get a fix on his general location, we can use you to smoke him out. Don't ask me anything more. You're not supposed to know even this much! Not yet anyway."

Frank pointed a finger at Huff and said, "Stay here!" Frank went out on the dock and Kimberly and Huff watched him. Frank stood still and was staring out across Lake Washington. Dark clouds and rain were marching across Lake Washington and Frank retreated to the house before the rains arrived. The afternoon light dimmed with the arrival of the rain and the house lights were turned on.

• • •

On a previous visit, Huff had brought along Sandy Peck. She was voluptuous, a charmer, and supposedly his sixteen year old daughter. Again, Huff brought Sandy Peck. After the usual and expected pleasantries, Sandy, with Gator Aid in hand, had taken a seat out on the dock. Frank and Dennis Huff took seats on the back deck while Huff kept an eye on Sandy. He said, "She wants to be FBI when she comes of age."

Frank thought, *She's not putting on the solemn, intense persona of Huff and every other FBI Agent I ever saw*—this is a bullshit statement if I ever heard one—so why is Huff bullshitting me?

• • •

On a clear day Frank and Dennis Huff again made the Tiger Mountain run. After they reached the top, catching their breath, Huff said, "Frank, it's hard to put together. You have a history of violence and you're known as a shark in the business world, but you also had a reputation as a good father. Could you address this contradiction?"

"That is not a contradiction. I protected and provided for my family, same as my grandfather did, the best I knew how. I knew Eddie Mackie from my school days and he was my real estate leg man. I may have been known as a shark in the business world but some of those in financial straits were damn glad to see me coming.

"Eddie Mackie's gay and was being picked on when we were kids. I put a stop to it. Later, he reciprocated, warned me that a rat pack was gathering to kick my ass after school. That was the time I took the baseball bat out of my locker and bat in hand—I made a run at them, scattered them, and for that I was expelled.

"I wasn't close to anyone in my school days, but Eddie and I were respectful of each other. Eddie's good at running down how much is owed on a property and other financial information. We would make an educated guess as to how much the seller would need to clear before they would sell. Then we'd make an offer. The real estate market was volatile, tricky, but when we got it right it was damn profitable."

"Rich kids, growing up in an affluent society, seem to assume that the fates will continue to smile on them—always have, always will, while kids like Eddie and me grow up knowing that hard times are just around the corner."

• • •

Frank flashed back on the halcyon days before the Adele Yonkey case was revived. That was when Natalie took the plunge. She enrolled at the University of Washington, signed up for an ambitious academic program, and loved every minute of it. Natalie was totally focused and while basketball took a backseat to Natalie's studies, she still remained the team's top player.

Eddie and Frank sat down with Natalie and gave voice to their concerns about the real estate market. Natalie listened, nodded, and said, "I'm going to look into it." She queried Frank and Eddie with a variety of suppositions, asked for feedback and spent more than a year, night and day, gathering facts and figures. Her analysis of these facts and figures demonstrated the how, the why, and the when of the real estate meltdown to come.

Natalie's research paper earned her a Doctorate in Economics, foreshadowed her career as a bank executive, and forewarned Frank and Eddie to get out while the market was still high. After the crash Frank picked up several properties at a pittance.

• • •

Frank was notified of a Texas Hold'em Tournament in ten days. He said, "Reserve me a seat. I'll be there." Then, feeling he could use some time alone to clear his head, he decided to leave early, drive slow, and take his time on the trip to Las Vegas. Driving down Highway 84 gave him time to think. He understood his father's surrender to a higher power, since that surrender was what was keeping him sober and out of prison, but he asked himself, *how can Melina and Wassef, so well educated, so intelligent, and without an ax hanging over their heads*—how can they believe in that fairy tale of a spook up in the sky? He struggled with the thought of how they could believe while he couldn't and he had no answer to that question.

Then Frank forgot to dim his lights for an oncoming car. Still, they dimmed their lights for him anyway. *Why did they do that for me when I didn't do it for them?* He checked it out two more times and each time he failed to dim his lights for oncoming traffic they still dimmed their lights for him. *What is it,* he thought, *that in this world prompts people to dim their lights for me*— even when I fail to dim my lights for them?

Even though Frank recognized the serenity that the religious experience afforded the true believer, having others dim their lights dim for him was as close as Frank ever came to having a religious experience. Sad.

CHAPTER TWENTY-THREE—Frank Meets The Moose

There had come a day when Frank and his father entered a small café. Four guys his dad's age were sitting together at a table. Passing, David said, "Friends of Bill W?" They grinned and nodded.

Frank turned to his Dad, "Friends of Bill W?"

""Means they're in AA." Later, David said. "I can't figure out how you always manage to spot a game."

"Same way you spot Friends of Bill W."

• • •

Stopping for gas and a cup of coffee in Boise, Frank found a game in progress. He took the game for about three hundred. On leaving he passed a six foot four bearded mountain of a man who weighed in at two sixty-five. He was at the time slightly drunk and engaged in amiable banter with a smaller man. When Frank passed, the mountainous one stepped behind him and reached his arm around Frank's neck. Frank grabbed his little finger and ripped it back full-force, tearing the tendons while freeing himself. The big man howled—he was game but Frank hit him with a left hook that rocked him and then with a right that cracked ribs. Several more punches, and like a tree falling in the forest, the big man tottered, and then gathering speed, he crashed to the floor.

• • •

When the police and the ambulance arrived Frank learned that the mountainous one was Vlad Rezak, a middle-aged con on Parole and better known as The Moose.

It seemed to Frank that he had heard that name before. He called his father who gasped

"I can't believe it! You running into The Moose. Frank, get the hell out of there and don't give the cops a statement. Go!"

Frank went into the men's room, opened the window and bailed out. A block away and inside the gas station, he handed the attendant a twenty and said, "I need to make a call."

David Grady picked up the phone on the first ring. "I can't believe it . . . you running into The Moose. I was a fresh fish in prison when Moose cut in the line in front of me. Big as he was, I said 'Moose, I can't let you punk me out. You cutting in front of me says that somewhere along the line, I'll have to cut you or fuck you up some other way. So why don't you cut in front of the punk behind me . . . that would save us both the trouble. Moose's eyes got big, he started laughing, and cut in front of the punk behind me. From that moment on we were friends.

"Moose was the best cellie I ever had. We shared the same cell the last three years of his sentence. Moose had a six year run on the outside before he came back. That was four years before my parole. The cops will want a statement. Be confused, contradictory."

Frank said, "Damn it Dad, you're guilt-tripping me. So now I'm supposed to feel bad about punching out some asshole? Okay, okay. I'll muddy the waters a little."

And that Frank did.

• • •

The next day Frank visited the hospital. There was a pay phone in the lobby and he called his father. David assured him that Moose is always acting and can come across as the friendliest bear in the forest. He can also be a pretty scary guy, but *he's never as crazy as he acts.*

Entering the room Frank said, "Moose, you did time with David Grady. He's my father."

"David Grady's your father. I'll . . . be . . . damned! He told me he had a son."

"Yeah. The doctors tell me those torn ligaments need the surgeon's touch. I'm getting you the surgeon and I'm paying for it. The nurses are pretty, especially that red-headed one, so you can stretch out and enjoy your stay. That'll give me time to talk to your PO and take full responsibility for what happened."

Moose said, "Why?"

"My Father."

"Uh huh."

• • •

Frank paid Moose's Parole Officer a visit. He was an overweight black man known by the nickname 'Rotten Ralph,' a man who granted no slack and would violate you in a heartbeat. With raised eyebrows, Rotten Ralph said, "Why you doing this?"

"On the inside my father and Moose were friends. Dad's clean and sober now, drives a forklift, and attends an AA meeting every day. Plus, I'm the one put Moose in the hospital."

Rotten Ralph growled, "I hate do-gooders! God, how I hate do-gooders—but you don't much look like a do-gooder. Show me some ID, give me the particulars on your father, his PO, everything. I make no promises, but I'll look into it and you'll hear from me."

• • •

Two days later Rotten Ralph visited the hospital. "Moose, you caught a break. I'm not violating you, but on your next conviction you'll probably get life. When you're ready to travel you'll be given a bus ticket to Seattle and you will report to PO Wendy Shothammer.

• • •

Moose's reputation in criminal circles is that he's good muscle and a good wheelman. Once settled in Seattle he took a job driving cab. The cabbies usual tips and clips were enough to live on but Moose was not happy. As part of the condition of his parole, Moose had to attend three AA meetings a week, and David Grady took Moose to his first AA meeting. The man chairing the meeting beamed goodwill and acceptance while Moose stood glowering in the back of the hall. For the last speaker the Chairman asked Moose if he would like to share with the group.

Moose snarled—"Hey! Don't you come at me all accepting! I'll throw you right through the fucking window!" Moose then pointed a finger at the brother who was moving in his direction and said— "And you'll go through the second window!"

The Chairman, still beaming acceptance, said, "Thank you for sharing. Now we'll close the meeting in the usual way."

When the meeting closed, one of the group rushed up to Moose and said—"Wow! That was great!"

Moose growled, "What's so fucking great about it? I just threatened to throw someone through the fucking window!"

"Yeah! That's what's so great. Up to now I've been the group asshole. Now *you're* the group asshole!"

Moose caught his breath. No one, on the bricks or in the joint, had ever come at him like that. He didn't know what to do.

• • •

After the meeting David and Moose stopped for coffee. Moose was confused and silent. Midway through that first cup of coffee his mood changed. He chuckled and said, "Those guys know where it's at." Grinning, Moose then started flirting with the waitress.

That was the beginning of the end for Moose's persona as a dangerous guy. Moose had decided that he liked these people.

• • •

Moose had been clean and sober for a solid year. He was out having coffee with members of his Home Group and noted Don Chaffee was silent as he drew on his cigarette and sipped coffee. Moose said, "Don, what's up?"

Don sat down his cup. "We've got this kid Roland in the Treatment Center. When he came in he was so messed up on drugs and alcohol that I thought he was brain damaged. Now he's beginning to track and think straight but no way is he ready to leave treatment. His mother and his girlfriend are coming down tomorrow to pull him out of treatment and he's going to die."

Moose dropped his chin down on his clasped hands. There was a silence as Moose leaned back and thought on it. Gently, he said, "Mind if I be there?"

• • •

Moose was sitting in the lobby when Roland's mother and girlfriend showed up. He looked on them with indifference. Roland arrived accompanied by Don and another Staff member. Moose noted she was an attractive woman his age and her name was Thelma.

Don and Thelma were advising Roland to stay, while his girlfriend and his mother were telling Roland he didn't need to be there, and that he should leave with them. The young man said, "I feel like I'm being pulled apart."

His mother dropped her eyes to the floor and reminded the assemblage that Roland was all she had left, that she had already lost her first son to suicide.

Moose lifted his head and said, "That is so fucking sad. Wanta try for two?"

All were startled. Moose, sounding bored, broke the silence. "Oh come on—You know you need the action—In the joint we see it all the time. I did twenty years and we love the smother love you drop on your kids. You send us kids with no balls at all. My last Jenny was like that. He came into the joint all scared and all I had to do was look concerned and say that he probably didn't need to go in there, that it wasn't safe for him in there. All I had to do was blow in his ear. He was grateful and wanting my protection he became my bitch. Perry had a sweet ass, washed my underwear, and if I needed anything like a pack of smokes I could always pimp him out. When Perry's time was up he blubbered and said, 'You've been just like a mother to me.'"

Roland shouted, "Hey! Fuck you!" Roland's mother reached out a hand and Roland slapped it away shouting, "And fuck you too!" He then charged back to the dorm.

When mother and girlfriend had vacated, Thelma stared at Moose. "Was that true?"

"The stories true only it wasn't me did the twenty and pimped out Roland. Hell, I don't even smoke."

"You," Thelma said, "are a sly old con man."

He beamed at her saying, "Thank you." Looking to Don, Moose said, "Professional complements are always welcome."

Thelma's mouth dropped open and she began to laugh.

• • •

Around Moose things were always happening.

He picked up a passenger at the bus station who said, "Drop me off at the nearest bar with live music." The passenger, on seeing the AA slogans Moose had posted in his cab said, "You a friend of Bill W?"

"Yeah. Wanta go to a meeting?"

"Uh. I guess so."

Moose drove his passenger to a meeting up on what is sometimes called pill hill, parked the cab across from the hospital and said, "Okay pal, this time the ride's on me. Come on. Let's go catch the Meeting."

• • •

David Grady, along with Moose and Thelma Hindenlang, met to have coffee with retired Parole Officer 'Rotten Ralph' Harding. Thelma, red-haired, green-eyed, and with big freckles, was sitting in the booth between Moose, the ex con, and Ralph, the ex Parole Officer. Moose grinning and Ralph not smiling but with a twinkle in his eye, were competing with each other to win Thelma's attention . . . and she loved it.

David Grady, watching this byplay, suddenly exclaimed, "I'll be Damned! I always knew Moose was an actor, but now I see 'Rotten Ralph's an actor too! When Moose violated his Parole by getting drunk and strong-arming my son, I wondered, how come Rotten Ralph didn't violate The Moose and send him back to the joint?"

The mask came off. "Grady, once you got off the sauce, since you lived with the urge every day, it was easier for you to see it coming. Moose was a binger. He would go for months not even wanting a drink and then, Bam, without warning the urge would take over— Moose would fall off the wagon—the drink would fall off the table."

Thelma was looking at Ralph. She saw the man beneath the

façade and fell in love with that man. So now she had that cozy feeling; she was in love with Rotten Ralph, with The Moose, and both of them wanted her. She hugged herself and thought, *things couldn't be rosier.*

Moose said, "Dave, you got me plugged into the AA Program and last week, when I ran into that rat bastard Poletti, him having snitched me off for a suspended sentence, and me then doing the nickel, instead of capping the bastard like any solid Con would do, I forgave him . . .. This AA Program can sure screw up your head."

David Grady, solemnly shaking his head, said, "Ain't that the truth Moose. *Ain't that the truth!"*

Thelma's mouth dropped open. Then she realized they were putting her on. Rotten Ralph and Thelma started laughing.

Grinning, Moose pointed a finger at Ralph and said, "Nailed your ass!"

No one but Moose could ever report having made Rotten Ralph laugh.

CHAPTER TWENTY-FOUR—Frank is Shot

Doc Frakowick would have lunch with Frank whenever he returned to Las Vegas. During lunch, Frakowick invited Frank to sit in on a hospital staff meeting. Doc said, "I'd like your feedback. There's a good deal of dissension going on within the staff. Everybody's suspicious of everybody. It's like a virus going around; we're experiencing a meltdown into paranoia and the source of this particular virus remains unclear."

Frank was at the meeting but he didn't listen to the complaints; they meant nothing to him—but he watched. Everyone who spoke looked angry and irritated . . . Except for the silent one in the back.

After a time, Frank whispered to Frakowick, "Who's the rat standing in the back?"

Doc said, "Who're you referring to?"

Frank identified the short dumpy woman he recognized as secretly enjoying the dissension.

Doc said, "Ah yes! Miss Withers. Everybody's confident—I've been so focused on the speakers and their complaints that I never noticed—*now it comes clear.*"

"They need a focus for their anger."

"And I'll give them that. *Watch me.*" Doc took the floor and in what he made look like an afterthought, Frakowick said, "Before I begin, let me voice my appreciation for Miss Withers hanging in with the agency while it's going through these troubling times. Always, she's been there for us, for all of us."

He chastised the others for not following the example of Miss Withers who "never said an unkind word about anyone." Then he said, "Miss Withers. Would you be willing at this time to share with us how you've managed to survive so many staff upheavals, remained friends with *everyone* and managed to avoid *ever taking sides?*"

Someone snickered, someone from the other side of the room also snickered, and a wave of recognition rolled through the room. Now they knew who they were angry with.

With a grim look that was far from friendly, Frakowick said, "What I'm hearing Miss Withers, is that you have fomented discord by taking *everybody's* side."

• • •

Doc Frakowick said, "Frank, you got shot in an earlier Vegas trip. How did that come down?"

"That was my first million dollar poker tournament. At that time my money was tied up in real estate and I didn't have the loose $100,000 needed to buy into the game. Artie Karp had seen me around and had monitored my play in other games. In my early Las Vegas days Artie put out a feeler to see if I would come in with him as a member of his crew. I had thanked him for the offer—told him my plate was already full."

"On this occasion Artie said, 'Frankie, if you're willing, I'll put up the front money and we'll split whatever you win.'"

"Texas Hold 'em's not my best game. I could lose."

"If you lose then you say nothing about my having put up front money and you walk away as if nothing happened."

"My instinct said there was something chancy in the air, but my head overruled. Self-will was running wild; I wanted in that game so I took up Artie's offer. My head was telling me I had everything to gain and nothing to lose. My head was wrong."

There were nine others in the game. Frank, Chigger, and Fast Eddy were the professionals. Three of the players, Ricco, Big Tami, and Harry the Lip, were mob guys, three were Texas oilmen, and one was a TV star. A large group of spectators were on the rail and a million in chips was on the table.

Ricco was an animated sort of guy and yet Frank recognized Ricco taking a five-ten second moment of stillness to savor the moment. He won that hand big. When Ricco did not have a sure winner that brief moment of stillness was missing. On one of his hands on the blind Frank had nothing and folded. He figured Chigger had opened and bet high on a medium level pair (Jacks or Queens) to narrow down the field. On the flop the only related cards were the six and seven of clubs along with the jack of hearts. Chigger checked. This told Frank that Chigger had improved his hand and didn't want to scare away the others by raising.

Ricco again had that moment of stillness, but this was *before* he was dealt the last card giving him the winning hand.

Frank was convinced Chigger would have three Jacks. On the River another Club was turned, Chigger checked, and Ricco bet high. Chigger re-raised him. On the showdown Ricco beat three jacks with a back door flush in Clubs. Ricco had known he would be catching a back door flush—the collusion of Ricco and the dealer had knocked Chigger out of the game.

In the early days dealers sometimes colluded with a player to provide them with the winning hand. With modern surveillance techniques cheating by the dealer had all but disappeared and yet Frank recognized that the dealer and Ricco were working together. Frank did not want to break that up—not yet anyway. He wanted to isolate Ricco and play him head to head.

So for the next four hours Frank played to survive rather than to win. Within that time eight players had been knocked out. Only Ricco and Frank were left. Frank called for a new dealer—and the blood drained from the dealer's face.

Frank still had $65,000 in front of him when he and Ricco went head to head.

Rattled, Ricco lost good judgement. He had an Ace showing and raised Frank all his chips. Frank thought Ricco was bluffing, and it took guts, his having only a pair of Kings, but Frank called, and that was the decisive hand. With winning that hand, Frank had almost $130,000 in front of him. Ricco lost his cool and Frank could then read him like a book. In only six more hours he cleaned out Ricco Juliano. It was on that night that Frank developed into a first rate

Texas Hold 'em player.

When he won the hand that cleaned out Ricco there was much letting out of breath and applause from the spectators for an exciting game. There were also those who had figured out that Ricco and the first dealer had been in cahoots.

Frank had become involved in an ongoing mob power struggle and Artie Karp came forward and shook Frank's hand. Frank returned Artie's front money, and they split the rest down the middle.

Big Tami and Harry the Lip, the other two mob guys, came forward. Big Tami said,

"Thanks, I didn't know Ricco could be a rat."

Having now shown this kind of disrespect for other mob guys, Ricco was a dead man walking.

• • •

On an earlier run up Tiger Mountain, Huff had said to Frank, "Try this run with a thirty pound pack on your back."

Arriving for this run up Tiger Mountain, Frank surprised Huff by taking two thirty pound packs out of his trunk.

Grinning, Huff said, "You bastard!"

Frank had secretly trained for this moment. They damn near killed each other with neither man giving in on that run. Frank threw up twice, was only four steps behind Huff when they reached the top, his left leg had begun to flop, he was one sick puppy, and Huff wasn't much better.

It was going to be a long break before they started back down. Looking out over the south side of the mountain, Huff said, "I can't get over it. You beat that game for almost $600,000, were able to keep almost half of that, and then you got shot."

"Damn sure did! This all happened before you FBI came after me. I wired my winnings to my Seattle account and the following morning I checked out of my room, drove to the edge of town, and stopped for breakfast. On leaving the diner, in some way, I knew someone was coming up behind me and I was halfway through my turn when I received a blow to my right side that knocked me down. Knowing I'd been shot I rolled over on my back, pulled my left leg up to my chest, and pulled the thirty-eight from my ankle holster. Another shot went through the inner side of my left leg and entered my gut."

Already going into shock, Frank wrapped both hands around his revolver, aimed and got off two shots—one shot had put a bullet through Ricco's heart.

Huff said, "Being shot—God I know the feeling! But even shot through the heart, it's not instant death. Ricco still had time to get off another shot. If it had been me—I would've got off another, possibly two shots. Definitely, I would have taken you with me."

• • •

When Frank had returned to consciousness, there was a figure in green bending over him. He tried to speak but no words came out . . .. He drifted off.

The surgeons had been called on to do a good bit of patching up of intestine and stomach. It made for a long surgery.

• • •

Frank came out of the fog three days later. His dreams had been awful. He was having trouble getting his eyes focused, was in considerable pain, but he was alive. Melina, while having little experience with gunshot, had taken up residence on a fold-out cot placed in his room and monitored his vital signs. She had been present when he came out of the fog. Frank was no fan of pain and they put him on a morphine drip.

• • •

When Frank was stabilized, Captain Roskie paid a visit. Roskie wanted to know what Frank remembered.

"I must've seen or heard something that clued me in that someone was coming up behind me. I wheeled about, Ricco hurried his shots—must've been about twenty feet away—I'd been going to the shooting range twice a week the last four years and was the better shot."

Captain Roskie thought about it for a moment, grunted and exclaimed, "Oh Hell! I know what you saw Frankie! It was a stolen car backed into the parking space. That car hadn't been there when you parked. You hadn't seen the driver so he had to be behind you! Ricco had come at you with a thirty-eight with a silencer."

When Captain Roskie mentioned the car backed into a parking space Frank saw in his mind's eye a picture of that car. He said, "It was a late model white Ford."

Roskie said, "We found the first dealer in a ditch. Twenty-two caliber gunshot to the back of the head."

• • •

Having begun Physical therapy, when he was wheeled back to his room, Frank found Artie Karp waiting for him.

"Damn Artie! You sure did get me into something!"

"Yes I did. I thought Ricco would come after me and I was ready for him. But him being the rat bastard he was, he came after you instead."

"Who else'll be coming after me Artie?"

Solemnly and with finality, Artie announced, "No one. I returned the money the two Wiseguys lost, and the Casino reimbursed Chigger, Fast Eddy, the Texas oilmen, and the TV actor. In the mob it's a matter of honor to never back down. You've never backed down in your life, something we admire. And since you'd already made your bones by killing Ricco, me and the others Ricco had cleaned out, we saw to it that you became an 'honorary' Made Man. That's never been done before."

"What's it mean?"

"It means, Artie said, "That no mob guy can make a hit on you without consent from the Council. I've taken care of the medical bills, did it in cash and in your name, so you can take the medical expenses off your Income Tax. You ever need anything, you let me know."

• • •

When Frank grew stronger he was transported to the airport, flown to Seattle, and on a dark and rainy night, an ambulance returned him to his home.

The FBI paid Frank a visit. "We hear you're now a Made Man."

Frank said, "Not! You heard wrong!"

CHAPTER TWENTY-FIVE—The Recruitments

Matty Helms had broken out of Juvenile Detention. He preferred daytime burglaries when everyone was at work and the house was in a secluded area. Perfect.

Cold and hungry, Matty put a frozen TV dinner in the microwave before his search of the upper floors. He located a handful of change and a warm coat too large before sitting down to eat.

Before leaving he checked the basement again. There had been a padlocked door down there. Why? Matty found a crowbar and pried off the lock. Feeling along the wall he found the light switch. Turning on the light Matty exclaimed, "Oh shit!" A naked girl was chained to the wall. "Hang on Sis. I'm going to get you out of this!"

Matty called 911 and said, "I was burglarizing this house when I found a girl chained to the wall in the basement. She's in bad shape— I've got a crowbar and if this bastard gets here before the cops I'll cave his fucking head in!"

Matty hung up the phone and wrapped the freezing girl in a blanket and gave her a drink of water. She drank some but was unable to speak. Her back and butt Shad been striped with ugly raw welts and they were infected. "The cops, he said, "will be here any minute so you hang in there." Matty picked up the crowbar and headed up the stairs.

A Cruiser with a male/female team arrived. Matty laid down

the crowbar and led the way. The ambulance pulled in, the girl was freed, placed on a stretcher and loaded into the ambulance. Her name was Myrna Pellegrini.

When the Ambulance pulled out Officer Bradden said, "Son, you did a good thing. I'm sorry, but I have to cuff you."

"Don't worry about it. I can always bust out again."

. . .

The house belonged to Secret Service Agent Don McKee. He was on a flight from Miami back to DC after a two day assignment.

Stewardesses always smile. Usually the smile is genuine—but when stressed-out, sick, or hung-over, they will still force a smile. Don McKee was sitting in a seat on the aisle while one of the Stewardesses was forward and huddled in conversation with the co-pilot. She looked back and into Don McKee's eyes—then looked away. Her smile was forced as she walked down the aisle reminding everyone to fasten their seat belts. Prior to that huddled conversation her smile had been genuine and spontaneous. McKee noted this.

The plane was on the ground and waiting for instructions to taxi to the Off-Loading Gate. Don McKee knew how to trigger the Emergency Exit, did so, slid down the chute and disappeared into the night.

. . .

Melina called from Switzerland. Frank said, "Why you calling? Are the kids okay?"

"They're fine. I have something to say. This is hard. My parents are here. We learned that you were never a suspect in the disappearance of the five women FBI Agent Eddy Addison told us about. That was the day before The Times published that FBI profile of a serial killer that was made to look like you. Frank, we are all so very sorry."

"Yeah! That was not good." Choking up, Frank handed the phone to Kimberly, retreated to the bathroom and locked the door.

Time passed. Kimberly knocked on the door, asking, "Are you alright?"

"Yeah. I'm okay." He unlocked the door.

Kimberly saw his stricken face and said, "Well . . . that was a long time coming."

Bewildered, Frank said, "I thought I'd got past it!"

• • •

The running path around Greenlake is level all the way. Frank, Kimberly, and Huff had completed two laps around the lake. They walked for a time to cool off and then relaxed on a park bench.

Frank said, "Huff, you've spent a lot of time scoping me out and picking Kimberly's brain about me. Now you need to do something for me. Unofficially, check to see if anything has happened to FBI Agent Eddy Addison."

"Huff looked at Frank . . . "Eddy Addison had a ticket to a Cubs game and was heading for his car when someone with a baseball bat fractured both his thighs. You going to tell me what's going on Frank?"

"No I'm not! Thanks, Dennis."

• • •

The unexpected death of Secret Service Director Hal Hendricks triggered an intense and clandestine political battle to determine who would emerge as the new head of the Secret Service. In the meantime, while the battle quietly raged, Agent Joanna Kickman was thrust into the position of Interim Director, and as such, she called Agent Dennis Huff to her office.

Kickman said, "I'd like to know why you quit the FBI and joined the Secret Service?"

"FBI Agent Eddie Addison convinced the mothers that Frank Grady was being investigated in the disappearance of five women. Truth is, Frank was never a suspect, was never in the area when any of the women disappeared. Also, the day after Addison laid that trip on the women, the newspaper printed a bogus profile of a se-rial killer. That profile fit Frank to a tee . . . that was it for me. The current FBI had poor leadership and I wanted out.

"Frank's curious about what we're up to, curious about our foxy little juvenile delinquent Sandy Peck and that, plus his relationship with Kimberly Wheaten, would seem to be the only things holding him here."

"Huff, when the present political dust settles, I will be replaced with a new Director, but in the meantime—I'm in position to advance your career."

• • •

Retired Detective Phil Baade had interviewed Frank's former teacher Mrs. Baxter, who began her tenure as Principal shortly after Frank's expulsion. She retired when her husband became terminally ill. Phil Baade had also lost his mate to cancer. Looking on Phil critically, Mrs. Baxter said, "Are you by chance a drinking man?"

Sighing, Phil replied, "I was a moderate drinker until my wife became ill. Since that time I've been drinking more than I should . . . more than I even like."

Phil, admiring Mrs. Baxter, promised himself that after concluding this case he was going to get off the sauce, quit smoking, and come back and see this lady.

Mrs. Baxter asked, 'Would you like coffee or perhaps tea?"

"Coffee black would be fine."

There was something in Phil's manner that allowed Mrs. Baxter to trust him. She reported, "For a time Frank Grady had been friends with Wayne Phillips and Alex Fischer, and each of them had been exceptional in different ways. Wayne Phillips was confident, good looking, and popular, Alex Fischer was artistically talented and his freehand drawings were much admired while Frank was recognized as being the strongest, toughest kid in the school. What was not recognized was that Frank was also the smartest kid in the school."

Mrs. Baxter poured the coffee. "Probably the most deliberately malicious act I ever saw in my years of teaching occurred shortly after the summer vacation.

"Frank had punched out Jumbo Cummings, a true bully who had made life hell for Eddie Mackie and other gay kids, and for a brief time this made Frank the Golden Boy, the Golden Boy who clothed himself by late night crawls into the Goodwill drop-off box. Wayne Phillips had been the Golden Boy and responded to his loss of Kingship by persuading Alex Fischer to draw an illustration of Frank Grady in tattered clothing with elbows and knees sticking out through holes in the clothing, with the soles of his shoes flopping down, and with his toes sticking out of the shoes. The sketch was well-done, and with the split-scar on Frank's lip and his broken nose being exaggerated in the drawing, it made Frank clearly recognizable."

Phil said, "Mean."

"Copies were made and circulated around the school. Frank recognized that only Alex could have executed the drawing while he was unaware of Wayne's part in goading Alex to do the drawing."

Frank took down the copy taped to his locker, confronted Alex and said, "Alex, I can't let you get away with this. You have to eat the drawing." Alex demurred so Frank knocked him down and said, "You're going to eat this drawing or I'll stomp you to pieces."

Alex started eating the drawing. When he chewed and swallowed the first piece Frank walked away.

• • •

Huff and Frank were watching the Seahawks game on TV and on this day the Seahawk offense was misfiring.

Kimberly entered the room and served coffee. When she exited Huff said, "The Secret Service is considering your unique skills for an upcoming operation. They will come looking for your help. You might consider not telling them to fuck off. Never forget the Government is not pleased with your seduction of former FBI Agent Kimberly Wheaten. Also, almost to a man, they're convinced you orchestrated the death of Agent Tom Nichols. It's believed, that in the cases of Agent Tom Nichols, you got away with murder."

"That's bullshit."

"You know it, I know it, but they don't know it. Still, they need you. My superiors have informed me that if you bend a knee they'll bend a knee."

Frank paused . . .softly he said, "I'll . . . be . . . damned! I knew there was *something*. You're not with the FBI anymore!"

"No I'm not. I'm with the Secret Service."

"I'll be damned." They arose from their chairs, shook hands and without another word Huff headed for the door. Opening the door he paused to look back saying, "You're an edgy kind of a guy Frank. We never know what you're going to do next."

CHAPTER TWENTY-SIX—On to Rio

Huff had not known, prior to being given the on-the-ground leadership role in the upcoming operation, that it was expected that Frank and the women would be fatalities. He was not pleased on learning this. He stormed, "Why in God's name are you so comfortable with the idea that Frank and the women will die in this operation?"

Director Kickman raised her eyes up from the floor, and said, "Huff, that's not the plan but that's probably what'll happen. I'm as troubled by this as you are . . .. "It's former Secret Service Agent Don McKee. He's the best ever. Frank Grady's smart and tough but he's older and doesn't stand a chance against this guy. In our training sessions we all came to recognize that Don McKee was way, way ahead of the rest of us.

"You will be monitored electronically, and when Frank and the women meet with Don, since we know Frank will fight and we know he's a hard man to kill, hopefully, you will arrive in time and in enough force to save the women and take down Don McKee. We need him alive—we need to know more about that organization, who they are and how they recruited Don."

• • •

The day came when Agent Kickman paid Frank a visit. Seeing

her, Frank said, "You're the cop in the loaner car who asked me for directions."

Kickman and Frank stood naked to each other in Frank's doorway. "We need," Kickman declared, "you and Kimberly to flush out a rogue Secret Service Agent. He's good—a well-trained professional assassin."

"Why me?"

"Because he's good. The best I've ever seen. Don McKee's into BDSM, that's Bondage/Discipline & Sado/Masochism. He prefers girls in their early teens. He puts them in bondage—uses and tortures them—then they die. We need a teenager and Kimberly to travel with you to Rio de Janeiro as your Bondage/Submissive slaves. We know Don will be arriving in Rio shortly. We would like having you in place when he arrives."

"Why not have your own people in place?"

"Because Don knows most of our faces and do you think any of us, even those he doesn't know, could bring off such a masquerade? Don would recognize another agent in a heartbeat. When we think about who could pull this off we think of you."

"All the crap you Government people put me through, you harassed me and my family for years, you tore my world and my family apart and now you have the gall to ask for my help. God! You amaze me."

Agent Kickman was saying nothing.

Frank looked up and said, "Don't let the door hit you in the ass on your way out."

Kickman left saying, "I'll get back to you."

• • •

Mister Wassef Hamdi had uncovered the plot to assassinate the President-Elect prior to his being sworn in as President. Chaos would then reign in the Oval Office.

• • •

The next day Agent Kickman returned with Wassef Hamdi and Dennis Huff. Wassef said, "Hear us out Frank. The plan calls for you to take a vacation in Rio de Janeiro with Kimberly and a young girl and both posing as your Bondage Slaves."

"I'm not into that lifestyle, I know about it and I don't want it. Plus, I have no intention of recruiting a young girl."

Dennis said, "That's all been taken care of."

"Dennis. I don't believe you'd put your own daughter at such risk . . . and I never bought it that she was your daughter."

"I didn't think you did—but you went along with it as if you did. You're right; she's the most cunning, experienced, and charming little crook any of us will ever meet." Then Dennis Huff dropped his eyes.

Seeing this it came to Frank that they suspected he would not survive. He looked at Dennis and quietly said, "You *knew* about this?"

Dennis shook his head. "Not until five days ago. That was when I was selected and briefed as the one to lead the ground detachment."

Frank looked to his ex-father-in-law who said, "Unlike the others I rate you a 60-70 percent chance of surviving."

Kickman continued, "When we think about who could bring off a masquerade as a sadist and at the same time protect the women we think of you. The Agents we've considered, they couldn't pull it off—and that is why you're needed—there's no one else."

"Also you don't want one of your own getting killed."

Kickman nodded and said, "That too."

"Uh huh. Child Protective Services are snooping around so my children and their mothers can't come back to the States—and still you're asking for my help?"

Joanna Kickman conceded, "We'll quash that investigation. Do this and we'll make it safe and bring them home." Kickman dialed up a number on her cell-phone saying, "Send her in."

Sandy Peck came walking up the street and into the house. Wassef Hamdi, Director Kickman, and Dennis Huff took a walk out on the dock. Sandy was as Frank remembered, voluptuous to the point of exaggeration, accented by a small waist and well-rounded butt along with a facial expression that mirrored innocence and integrity.

This clever girl had cultivated and practiced her personal look of vulnerability and simple trust to perfection. The three of them took seats at the dining room table.

Sandy stated, "I know how I look. I'm the perfect bait for a predator who likes young girls. You're not getting a cherry in this operation. In my young life I've worked about every scam there is."

Kimberly and Frank stared at each other. Frank turned to Sandy and asked, "You know what would be expected of you?"

Calmly and with a hint of a smile Sandy said, "I've made four trips from Mexico City to San Diego with large containers of cocaine up my vagina and rectum. Then I traveled to other cities making my deliveries—I can take you in as well—and I can take a whipping. I have a legal driving permit dated from three years back stating I was then fifteen years old along with a birth certificate saying I'm now eighteen years old."

"This operation requires me to pose as your sex slave. I'm not someone who can get lost in a crowd and my upcoming trial as an adult will then go away." With a warm, open looking smile she continued . . . "who knows . . . I'm not your normal type girl and I might even like it."

Frank stood, walked out on his deck and stared at those on the dock. They recognized this as a signal to return.

Frank said, "You people are asking a lot. I have three kids, haven't seen them in a long time."

Huff directed a look at Frank's father-in-law.

"My daughter was pregnant at the time she left. You have a fourth child. Your son is named Wassef."

• • •

Frank lurched out of the house and down to the dock. He stood staring over the water while they watched and waited.

This day the surface waters of Lake Washington were still and smooth as glass. Whatever currents or turbulences were lurking below the surface remained non-visible. Calmly, and without a hint of turbulence, twelve minutes later, Frank walked back into the house and sat.

They watched. He was lost in thought. Lifting his head, they saw in his eyes an acceptance that he probably would not survive this mission. He said, "I'll see the women get out."

Director Kickman would later report, "Even then, I believed him."

Taking a deep breath Frank said, "The situation could arise where it will be necessary to demonstrate that this girl is my sexual submissive. I'll need a legitimate certificate of marriage and a prenuptial agreement putting a limit on the amount of money Sandy will receive at either the dissolution of our marriage or on my death. Annette Tyler is the Executor of my Last Will and Testament and this, along with the prenuptial agreement, needs to be attached to my will."

Agent Kickman said, "That will be arranged."

Sandy, Kimberly, and Frank were briefed. Kickman declared, "We don't know what Don McKee looks like now. We don't know who the plastic surgeon was, but we do know he had the surgery. How he was able to access and destroy his Secret Service records is a mystery that's still unraveling. What we have at present is an audio record of a talk he gave on security. It's enough. His voice is distinctive and his pronunciation is precise, very clipped, very anal. Familiarize yourselves with that tape and you will recognize that voice and that cadence even if he speaks only a few words in your presence."

• • •

Sandy, Kimberly, and Frank flew to San Francisco. Thelma Waltrip provided Kimberly and Sandy with a kink wardrobe, matching slave collars of silver chain fastened with silver locks, and wide silver wedding rings having two chain links attached. Then they flew to Mexico City where Frank and Sandy were married.

They were ready.

• • •

CHAPTER TWENTY-SEVEN—Meet Don McKee

On landing in Rio de Janeiro, a porter transported their luggage to the first taxi in line.

The bungalow was secluded and shaded while the courtyard was separated from the Alley by a five-foot-high cement wall topped with broken glass. A break in the wall enclosed a locked gate composed of vertical steel bars that allowed for a view into the courtyard.

Late afternoon, Frank put Kimberly and Sandy—nude, hands bound, ball-gagged, collared, and on leashes. When they heard laughing men walking down the alley. Frank said, "Okay girls, you're on." He led them out for a stroll in the courtyard. Those passing took advantage of the break in the wall. By the third afternoon, chairs were brought to stand on and peer over the wall.

The bungalow was also bugged.

Each mid-day Frank took Kimberly and Sandy in their thong bathing suits to the topless Abrica Beach. Welts were sometimes visible on their backs and butts.

• • •

The Secret Service tail was never allowed closer than a hundred yards. Seventeen days after their arrival, by cellphone, their tail reported having lost contact. Huff ordered his agents to spread out and relocate.

· · ·

The moment had arrived. While they were having cappuccinos at a sidewalk café, their quarry approached. Don McKee was accompanied by his teenage hostage. She was Spanish, beautiful, and her spirit had been numbed-out and broken. Frank looked her over. Eyebrows up, lips pursed, he nodded to Don in approval. Don looked over Frank's slaves and nodded in approval.

Sandy spoke a little Spanish and attempted to strike up a conversation with Don's hostage.

Frank commanded, "Cease!"

Sandy flinched and big-eyed responded, "Yes Master." Sandy and Kimberly dropped their eyes to their drinks.

Relaxed, Frank said, "We seem to share a mutual interest."

Nodding, Don McKee responded, "Perhaps we could get together sometime?"

When he spoke, Sandy and Kimberly recognized the voice of Don McKee, and being the thorough professionals that they were, they did not lift their eyes, but continued to stare into their drinks.

Frank said, "Would you care to join me for a cappuccino?"

The invitation was accepted and Frank looked over Don McKee's slave. He said, "I wouldn't mind playing with your slave for a change of pace."

"That could be arranged, and while we're at it I could probably show you a few tricks your slaves have never experienced."

Frank's eyebrows rose. "Interesting. My bungalow is about twelve blocks from here and I'm always on the lookout for something new."

"Shall we?"

Frank thought about it, nodded, said, "I think so."

Taking their time, both men finished their cappuccinos. Frank said, "Your slave, she's totally broken."

He sighed, "The breaking is a lot of fun, but once they're broken they're not as much fun anymore."

"Exactly." Frank said, "I like to leave mine with a spark. With a spark left, I never get bored."

Don conceded, "You do have a point."

Kimberly and Sandy followed four steps behind, each holding a wrist of Don's slave.

• • •

Agent Tony Selvan reported, "Got them! They have company! A guy and a young girl and they're headed back towards the bungalow."

Huff said, "Everybody go! Surround the bungalow, we'll let them get inside before we move in, and people, more than anything, we want this guy alive!"

The women entered the bungalow first. When Don McKee and Frank entered Kimberly had the dart gun in her right hand and concealed at her side.

Was that what Don saw when they entered? He slashed at Frank's throat while Kimberly fired the tranquilizer dart.

Rather than duck away, Frank had ducked his head down and in, and took the cut across his jaw and chin rather than his throat. Frank heard the blade grating on bone while he hit Don McKee with a solid left hook to the liver. Don McKee's knees gave way and he crumbled to the floor.

• • •

Blood was everywhere. Dennis Huff led the charge into the bungalow. Frank was what Huff called, "A frigging bloody mess."

Don's knife was serrated and as sharp as any scalpel—so sharp that initially Frank had not felt the cut. Don McKee was not in the habit of leaving witnesses.

Frank was sat in a chair while Sandy straddled his legs, had the back of his neck hooked in the crook of her left arm, and with her right hand she was pressing a towel against his face with all her might. Compression had slowed but not stopped the flow—and Frank and Sandy were covered with Frank's blood.

The medical team took over, worked on Frank while a barely conscious Don McKee was put in restraints and then into a packing crate. They delivered the packing crate to a waiting private plane.

Don McKee was no longer Huff's concern. Huff's responsibility was now to get the three women and Frank the hell out of there.

Frank was given a dose of morphine, his face was stitched, emergency style, and he was given a transfusion of plasma. Huff got Frank, Sandy, Kimberly, and Don McKee's former slave Wanda Duarte on a private jet standing by.

• • •

On the flight back to the States, Kimberly said, "Dennis, on our flight to Rio, I asked Frank about the report that he was responsible for the death of Tom Nichols."

Frank said, "I had assumed it was the profile published by the Seattle Times that frightened the women away, and that it was Tom Nichols who worked up that supposed Profile of a Serial Killer—I couldn't have been more wrong—I had wanted to give Tom a taste of what it feels like to have your children under attack while being helpless to protect them.

"Nichols had a fifteen-year-old daughter. She was a High School Cheerleader and I acquired a picture of the Cheerleader Squad and visited Tom Nichols with every intention of using that picture to fuck with his head, but I didn't do it."

"Why not?"

"Nichols informed me it was Director Alvin Frugate who worked up that bogus profile and fed it to the media. Then he told me how FBI Agent Eddie Addison had visited the women at my home on the day before that bogus profile was published. Addison had shown the women photos of women who had gone missing after supposedly meeting with me."

• • •

The Federal Prosecutor had said, "Frank, you left Agent Nichols, and twenty minutes later he had a massive seizure and died. You killed Agent Nichols, but there's not enough physical evidence to bring you to trial. How does it feel to get away with murder?"

Director Kickman pondered out loud, "Frank knew he was probably going to get killed if he took this mission. When McKee slashed at his throat, why did he duck his head towards the knife rather than away?"

Wassef Hamdi said, "Redemption. He doesn't care what the rest of us think, but he would like redemption in the eyes of the women and children . . . secondarily he wanted to save the two women, he's tired, worn out."

. . .

Two days after his plastic surgery, and after their arrival in DC, Frank was in his hospital room and going through the unpleasantness of a cold-turkey withdrawal off opiates. Kimberly Wheaten and Dennis visited him, were standing close together. Frank noted this and without moving his jaw, like a ventriloquist, he said, "Dennis, Kimberly wants to have children and I can't go the family route again. She wants you, you want her. What's standing in your way?"

"Her commitment to you."

"Forget that. The two of you do what you're going to do and just get on with it! I'm in the unpleasantness of a cold-turkey withdrawal so get out of here."

. . .

The next day Kimberly and Dennis returned. Kimberly said, "Frank, how you feeling today?"

"Better than yesterday."

"Dennis and I," Kimberly said, "want to get married."

He raised his hand saying, "You should. You're two of my favorite people and peace be with you both."

. . .

CHAPTER TWENTY-EIGHT—The Presidential Detail

Agent Joanna Kickman, thanks to the success of the mission she set up, was posted as the new Secret Service Director.

Don McKee had done a good job of breaking the spirits of Myrna Pellegrini and Wanda Duarte—and they were now Joanna Kickman's wards. Kickman said to Matty Helms, "Those girls are broken. You have not been broken and I'm assuming you have enough spirit for the three of you. I'm also assuming you're not prick enough to take advantage of them being in this state."

"You got that right."

"You think you could handle the task of standing up for and protecting the two women—even from yourself?"

Matty was stunned. Gathering himself he said, "Wow! This is the first time ever that I've been cast in the role of the good guy . . . Okay, yeah, I can do that . . . but they have that vulnerable look so don't be surprised if I have to kick some ass protecting them."

"That would not surprise me and in fact, them seeing you kicking ass to protect them might help restore their spirit. Time will tell."

• • •

Joe Renaurd, a Secret Service Trainer, was brought in to interview Sandy. Renaurd said "Sandy, if you were a Secret Service Agent and if you and your partner took someone into custody and they were carrying $10,500, if you saw your partner slip the $500 into his pocket, what would you do?"

"That's a slippery slope. I've been on a few of those already. In the past I would have found a way to end up with the money. What I'd do, this time around, is smile sweetly and then I'd turn the bastard in and I'd be asking for another partner. Let him talk his way out of that one!"

"Why," Renaurd said, "the difference?"

"There's no difference! It's the same game I've played all my life—only now I'm switching roles from one of the robbers to one of the cops. It's the game I love, the profit means nothing to me."

Joe Renaurd stared at Sandy for a good half minute before asking his second question. "If you were transporting a prisoner who was a mass murderer of young girls, and you came across an accident where a young woman needed your assistance to keep breathing and from bleeding out, and the mother of one of his victims drove up, recognized your prisoner, pulled a gun and was threatening to shoot him, what would you do?"

"How would I know she's one of the mothers? And she's waving around a gun? And I have a mass murderer in custody? Would I have to shoot her before she shoots me? All this while I'm transporting a mass murderer? I'm guessing now because I don't what I'd do. If I knew she was one of the mothers, I might be tempted to say, LATER! I need your help now to keep this girl breathing and from bleeding out! You can shoot the son-of-a-bitch later! I don't know what the hell I'd do. You have training protocols for dealing with things like this?"

Renaurd nodded, "We do."

• • •

Joanna Kickman said, "We're all in agreement that Sandy Peck is the most twisted, clever, and charmingly deviant 16 year old girl any of us will ever meet. God! That body coupled with that wholesome image, plus her being a stone criminal, she is unique. We'll never see another like her."

Kickman continued, "Frank, I've put my ass on the line and

you are now on the payroll as a Secret Service Agent. You screw up one time and then, as Director, I'm toast."

· · ·

Dennis Huff and Kimberly Wheaten came to say goodbye. Dennis was being reassigned to the President's Security Detail. Frank said, "You'll head that Detail one day."

Dennis said, "Probably. Frank, I have two questions. Why did you allow me all those interviews?"

"Parts of my childhood were pretty rotten . . . I chose to forget the bad parts but forgetting the bad parts lost me some of the connected good parts as well. You asking all those questions prodded me to remember some of the good parts I had lost."

"Second question—you knew we thought you probably would not survive if you found McKee, so why did you go through with it?"

"Don't know—What about McKee? What's with him?"

"Changing the subject? McKee was flown to an unidentified location somewhere in the Middle East. I believe he was rigorously interrogated. It was reported that shortly before he died he said, "I always knew it would come to this."

"Hah! He knew he was fated. So was I. Who my parents were, who my grandparents were, it shaped my life . . . I could either be ashamed or defiant. Maybe what I did will allow my kids to feel proud."

Before leaving, Kimberly bent down and kissed Frank. Huff stood at her side and said, "We'll just shake hands."

Frank rolled his eyes and said, "God I hope so! Take care you two."

CHAPTER TWENTY-NINE—Detective Baade

In college, Wayne Phillips had been popular with his Fraternity Brothers, popular with the coeds, and for a time, even with the Faculty.

Wayne succeeded in becoming engaged to Eunice Van Joines, one of the schools more attractive coeds. Her father owned and operated the Van Joines Real Estate Agency.

From the time Wayne Phillips had been a child, he had been attractive, charming, and popular. When they were in the seventh grade, briefly, before Frank wised up, Wayne had been popular even with Frank.

Prior to his marriage, Wayne confessed to his father-in-law-to-be that he was disillusioned with all the rah rah rah of college. He stated he was thinking of quitting; that he looked forward to getting real and joining the work force. His prospective father-in-law presumed that Wayne was eager to get to work and attributed to this personable and handsome young man a drive and work ethic that would lead to success. He offered Wayne a position as a Real Estate Agent with a decent salary plus the usual sales commission.

• • •

Wayne closed only two sales in over a year's time; he was a charmer, not a closer. His father-in-law said, "Wayne, if you worked half as hard at selling real estate as you work at selling yourself, you'd be a wonder. I pay you a decent salary and in 16 months you've closed only two sales. I keep waiting for you to find yourself but I can't afford you any longer. You're married to my daughter but you're fired."

Then Wayne was caught cheating on his pregnant wife.

• • •

Michael Moriarity was listening to Wayne regaling other customers with a humorous account of his travails when he said, "Wayne, you love the saloon atmosphere and the camaraderie. Bullshitting and being admired are the oxygen of your life. If this is what you want then you should get paid for it. Go get a job as a bartender."

• • •

One of Wayne Phillips's customers was a large, overweight, and lonely-looking gentleman who said his name was Fritz Tyler. Not seeking company, he preferred those times when he was the only customer, those times when he could watch the TV and drink alone.

Sometime after first coming around, while sitting at the bar and listening to the Nightly News, he heard TV reporter Buster Black refer to Frank Grady as still being a Person of Interest in a number of cases. The gentleman known as Fritz Tyler flew into a rage at the mention of the name Frank Grady. After that he proceeded to get drunk.

Before the customer became sloppy drunk and incoherent, Wayne asked him, "What is it about Frank Grady that has you so teed off?"

"Frank Grady's the bastard who ruined my life."

"How?"

"I was away from home looking for work when Frank Grady came along, seduced my teenage daughter, and turned my wife against me!"

"Not surprising," Wayne said, "I knew Frank Grady when we were kids. Even then he was a real bastard." Wayne then provided the customer with a free beer.

The customer known as Fritz Tyler looking blearily up at Wayne and said, "That son-of-a-bitch Frank Grady is too smart! No one, not me, not you, no one is ever going to hurt that son-of-a-bitch. He's laughing at us."

Wayne said, "He's not laughing because he didn't get away with anything."

The customer looked at Wayne questioningly.

Wayne explained, "Even if they never prove it the Adele Yonkey case is hanging over his head and will haunt him forever."

The customer looked puzzled. He finished his beer and left without another word.

• • •

The following early afternoon, the same customer arrived and stared at Wayne with a puzzled look—didn't speak, only stared.

Seeing this, Wayne laughed and said, "What?"

He said, "If he isn't laughing at us, then what is it?"

"I suspect that if he doesn't know why everyone's looking at him, then he's probably not going to feel like he's getting away with anything. Matter of fact, it would be driving him nuts trying to figure out what's going on."

The customer looked unconvinced.

"Just suppose," Wayne said, "that Adele Yonkey had an accident. Just suppose she fell and cracked her head. This is all hypothetical, and only between the two of us, but what if someone came along and saw this as an opportunity to set up an accident to look like a murder, and that Frank Grady was the perpetrator. Just think about how this would confuse him, be keeping him awake nights."

From under a knit brow, Wayne's favorite customer stared at him. Then the stare turned into a coy smile. Nodding, he said, "Oh! I like this."

• • •

In the days that followed the gentleman he knew as Fritz Tyler proved receptive to the idea that someone may have set up Frank Grady. For Wayne, it was nice knowing that someone appreciated all that Wayne had accomplished. Finally, someone he could confide in, who glowed with admiration each time Wayne parceled out information on how the finger could possibly have been pointed at Frank Grady.

. . .

Wayne described how someone could have made an anonymous phone call stating that on the day Adele Yonkey disappeared, he had witnessed Adele Yonkey getting in a car with Frank Grady.

The admiration elicited by Wayne's revelations prompted him to describe how the body of Adele Yonkey may have been set up to look like a sex crime. Wayne's admirer chortled with glee saying, "Oh! Wow! Frank Grady could be in a jackpot for a crime that never happened. This is priceless!"

. . .

Retired Detective Phil Baade paid a visit to the FBI Office in Seattle. After introducing himself, Phil said, "Frank Grady was the suspect in the Adele Yonkey case, and that case always bothered me."

"Why?"

"I met Frank when he was a troubled kid, followed his career, and I knew he never did the crime. Posing as Fritz Tyler, I taped conversations with Wayne Phillips. You need to hear them."

After listening to the tapes, Supervisor Dugan said, "He's guilty as hell but it's all circumstantial. We'll need more than this to convict."

"Adele Yonkey always wore a black onyx ring. When her body was found the ring was missing. Maybe he took it as a souvenir. Find him with the ring and that should do it."

Dugan nodded. Then he said, "What do you want out of this Detective Baade?"

"Bragging rights with other retired officers."

The FBI recovered Adele Yonkey's ring. It sat in a drawer next to Wayne's bed. Wayne Phillips was arrested for the murder of Adele Yonkey.

. . .

Frank and Sandy had come to Seattle for Wayne's trial. They were staying at the Olympic Hotel when Frank received a call from

Wassef Hamdi. "Frank, my daughter's heart took a turn for the worse. She's been checked into the Mayo Clinic, they don't have a heart for transplant, and Melina's not going to make it."

• • •

Sandy flew with Frank to Minneapolis where Frank rented a car and they drove to Rochester.

Melina's parents, were in the Waiting Room when Frank and Sandy arrived.

Dr. Hammond came pushing through the doors. "Are you Frank Grady, the husband?"

"I am."

"Her heart muscle has been so overworked by the valve damage that the muscle is mostly fiber. She's asking for you."

Frank staggered, then gathered himself.

"Nurse Edwards will take you to her."

• • •

Melina opened her eyes and saw Frank. She said, "You came."

He nodded, took her hand—so frail, so cold. He said, "All the crap you had to deal with."

"Not important now. We have two beautiful children. You take care of the children. All the children."

"I will."

"Thank you Frank—I want to say goodbye to my mother."

Frank walked blindly out of the room. Nurse Edwards led him back to the Waiting Room.

• • •

Frank and Melina's parents were at her bedside when, at 3:16 AM, Melina's heart stopped—no fanfare, no drama—it just stopped.

CHAPTER THIRTY—Wayne is Tried

As much as Frank would miss being with his children, including Wassef, the son he was seeing for the first time, it was agreed that, with the trial of Wayne Phillips coming up—this was not a time for him to take on the task of raising four traumatized children.

After Melina's Memorial Service, her body was returned to Egypt. Frank and Sandy returned to Seattle.

• • •

For some days Frank did not present himself at Wayne Phillip's trial. Phil Baade, being a witness, was there every day and kept Frank informed. Wayne's defense team could not dispute that it was Wayne Phillips who transported Adele Yonkey's body and posed her for discovery. What was in dispute was whether Adele's death was murder, an accident or was it manslaughter.

Against his attorney's advice, Wayne agreed to take the witness stand. In response to questioning by the Prosecutor, Wayne proclaimed, "I am not a murderer." Then he smiled at the jury and said, "I'm not that kind of a guy!"

The Prosecutor did not believe in bombast. Jurors listened more intently when things were stated without dramatics. He let Wayne's statement echo through the silent Courtroom. Pausing, and in keeping with the stillness that descended, the Prosecutor quietly and slowly repeated— "You're not that kind of a guy—We have your taped confession that it was you who phoned the FBI to say that Adele Yonkey was seen getting in a car with Frank Grady on the day she disappeared. Also, we have your taped confession that it was you who posed Adele's body for discovery. Let me see if I have this correct. Wasn't it your intention that Frank Grady would be indicted, convicted and sentenced to death?"

"I wouldn't have been responsible for that. It would've been the State!"

Someone in the Courtroom gasped at the sense of superiority now on display, the smugness, the extraordinary level of Wayne's narcissism, was now exposed. In the stillness of that moment, the Prosecutor raised his hands, palms up, and quietly stated, "I have no further questions at this time."

In the chill that descended on Wayne's defense team, they asked for a recess. Court was adjourned until the following morning.

• • •

Frank spoke with Defense Attorney Tim Skelly. Having nothing to lose since his Defense was already in the toilet, Tim agreed to call Frank Grady as a Witness for the Defense.

When Court was reconvened Tim Skelly stated, "I now call Mr. Frank Grady as a Witness for the Defense." The courtroom stirred. The Judge banged her gavel. Turning to the Prosecution she said, "This individual has not been listed as a Witness. Does the Prosecution have any objection to this witness?"

After a hushed conference, the Lead Prosecutor arose slowly. "Your Honor, this witness coming forward is a total surprise to us. Still, my colleagues and I will not object at this time."

Frank was seated in the witness chair and duly sworn in. Tim Skelly asked, "Mr. Grady, in your opinion, did Wayne Phillips actually plan and then murder Adele Yonkey?"

Frank replied, "I knew Wayne Phillips when we were kids. We were not friends and he didn't hesitate in his attempt to frame me for a murder I believe never happened. With no direct evidence pointing to him Wayne still managed to screw things up. Adele's death, like yesterday's testimony, had to be a miscalculation, manslaughter, a stupid accident. The Coroner reported that his first impression was that Adele Yonkey could have been struck hard enough that it may have left her unconscious and she may have fallen backwards and struck her head. I believe the Coroner got it right!

"Wayne Phillips did something stupid and Adele Yonkey died! It's my belief that Adele Yonkey's death was accidental and I wouldn't trust Wayne's account of that accident even for a minute."

The Prosecutor arose and calmly said, "Mister Grady, are you aware that our prisons are full of inept killers?"

"Can't say that I am. I've never been in prison."

With a nod of approval the Prosecutor said, "Touché Mr. Grady—Touché."

• • •

Attorney Tim Skelly worked a deal and the Prosecutor agreed to accept a guilty plea to the lesser charge of manslaughter.

Wayne Phillips' lifetime career was one of being well-liked and so he refused the plea bargain and he was dis-believing when the Jury then convicted him of First Degree Murder. As he was being led away he protested, "Wait, wait! This can't be! This is a mistake!"

• • •

Frank had lunch with Attorney Tim Skelly. Tim said, "After Wayne's sentencing, I reminded him that you are a hero to most outlaws and that you broke society's rules by living with more than one woman, defied the FBI, and you won. To those cons that makes you a hero."

Frank nodded. "Adele Yonkey was a modest young woman, yet Wayne not only killed her, but posed her in a way that was disrespectful of the person she was—Wayne feels nothing for others."

• • •

Sandy, returning from her shopping trip, saw Frank standing on the dock and looking out across the water. Ten minutes later she looked out the window and Frank still hadn't moved. She left the house, walked out to the dock and said, "Frank?"

It registered in Frank's mind that his name had been called and he turned.

"What's going on Frank?"

"Strange. I received a call from Annette and Natalie."

"What was strange about it?"

"I had wanted them and needed them, yet when they called and said they needed me, I realized that they needed me even more than I needed them. I turned them down the same way girls turned down my needy ass when I was a kid."

"What are you going to do Frank?"

"I don't know."

CHAPTER THIRTY-ONE—Closure

After the trial, retired Detective Phil Baade, along with Mrs. Alice Baxter, driving their Winnebago motor home, came to the Mercer Island home Frank had reopened. On seeing Mrs. Baxter, Frank thought he might know her. Mrs. Baxter smiled and said, "Yes Frank, It's me. I taught Math, second period."

• • •

Frank had not lived with Annette's cooking all those years without learning a few things. He and Mrs. Baxter prepared lunch.

After lunch, Frank said, "Mrs. Baxter, I always thought there was something screwy going on in that school. Was there?"

She nodded. "There was. Principle Pearson loved to pontificate. He would remind us teachers that Frank Grady was going to end up in prison, probably on Death Row, and that Wayne Phillips was the student most likely to succeed. Did that influence how some of our teachers related to you and other students? Unfortunately, it did!"

"I always knew something screwy was going on but I couldn't figure out what it was. You were OK, more than OK, but some of the other teachers really got down on me. Students then echoed the teacher's lead so I had no choice but to start kicking ass."

Turning to Phil, Frank said, "You're looking good."

"I stopped drinking, which was not so hard, stopped smoking, which was really hard, and while I'm never going to be slim, so far I've lost six pounds."

As a couple, Phil and Alice were both overweight, fond of literature, and fond of each other. Frank was happy for them. Before Alice and Phil continued on their trip down the coast, and possibly onto the Baja Peninsula, Phil said, "Who and what are you really Frank?"

"I had been a gambler . . .. Damned if I didn't try to be more. I got married, had children and played the role of a died-in-the-wool family man and legitimate businessman. I had thought I was home free and then it all fell apart. I became a Secret Service Agent, was injured, and am now pensioned off.

"For a long time nobody wanted me and now everybody wants me, even Annette and Natalie want me and my forgiveness. Walt Whitman said: Do I contradict myself? Very well then, I contradict myself. I am large, I contain multitudes."

"Trying to show off you're a literate man?"

"I don't know. Maybe I quoted Whitman to illustrate that we humans contradict ourselves—maybe I only want to lighten things up. My motives are suspect, even to me."

• • •

Phil Baade had belatedly determined that Wayne Phillips's claim of having been the one who called the FBI and reported having seen Adele Yonkey getting into Frank's car, had been a piece of bravado. Phil acquired a copy of that 911 call. He played it for Frank.

When the operator asked the name of the caller, Frank heard it when, in a froggy, disguised voice, the caller snarled, "Nero Wolfe," and hung up.

Hearing this, Frank knew. That left him with one more piece of unfinished business.

• • •

"What," Sandy said, "is going on Frank?"

"Annette and Natalie called again."

"What did they want this time?"

"They want me to take them and the kids back."

"You should, and when you do, I'll be moving on and with no regrets."

• • •

Frank was sitting in the dark in Eddy Mackie's house when Eddie entered and hit his light switch, no lights came on. He cursed.

Frank put the beam of the laser light on Eddy's left eye and said, "The beam is the sight for a Magnum handgun. Take a seat Eddy." After Eddy took a seat Frank said, "I see you still have the complete Nero Wolfe series. Archie Goodwin was Nero Wolfe's legman. I gave you work as my legman. You were good, no question, and we put together some sweet-assed real estate deals. When we were kids you warned me when a wolf pack was gathering to kick my ass. I always thought of you as the one friend I had from my school years.

"Why did you do this to me Eddie? Why did you call the FBI and say you saw Adele getting in my car?"

Eddy sighed. "I ran into Wayne Phillips down in Auburn. He said he saw Adele getting in your car on the day she disappeared. I asked him if he reported it. He said he didn't want to get involved, that there was no way he wanted Frank Grady coming after him.

"Adele had told me how much she regretted the way she treated you when we were kids. She felt guilty about the way she turned you down—said that set the tone for the way other girls would reject you. I thought Adele went to you to make amends and that you killed her. I loved Adele Yonkey about as much as any gay guy can ever love a woman."

"Huh. She was my first love too. It didn't go very well. If Adele and I had connected when we were kids, my life, and hers, would've been different."

Eddy asked, "Did she ever come to see you?"

"No, I never saw her, not once, from the time we were kids."

After a pause Eddy continued, "I was stunned to learn it was Wayne Phillips. I've been sick with regret and expecting a visit from you ever since. The FBI knew we did business together and came to see me. I told them it had been Adele's intention to go to you and make amends and they took it from there. Frank, what about your children and their mothers?"

"I've reopened my home on Mercer island. Annette and Natalie will be coming back and with the children. They'll arrive Thursday."

• • •

Frank and Eddie sat in stony silence. After maybe five minutes, Frank said, "There's no gun Eddie. The laser light is only a light. I pulled the main switch on your fuse box. You're being recorded and the tape recorder is sitting on the end table. You might want to get rid of it."

Eddy's breath whooshed out. "I thought for sure you were going to kill me!"

Frank walked to the door and said, "Not a chance. Have a good life Eddie."

He closed the door behind him.

It was over.

THE END

www.ingramcontent.com/pod-product-compliance
Lightning Source LLC
Chambersburg PA
CBHW071517100726
47908CB00004B/1199